Puppy Love

Sarah put the dog biscuit just inside the entrance to the badger set. A moment later, a little bundle of fur emerged, blinking nervously in the light. It was covered from head to feet with mud. Neil brushed the worst of it off from around its head and chest to reveal a dirty black and tan coat matted with dried earth. He could tell from the pup's teeth that it was very young, probably no more than seven or eight weeks old. It was also far too thin.

Neil scratched his head thoughtfully. "I can't understand how he got here. I wonder if he was a Christmas present that somebody didn't want?"

Titles in the Puppy Patrol *series*

More Puppy Patrol stories follow soon

Puppy Patrol
Puppy Love

Jenny Dale

Illustrated by

Mick Reid

A Working Partners Book

MACMILLAN CHILDREN'S BOOKS

Special thanks to Kirsty White

First published 1998 by Macmillan Children's Books
a division of Macmillan Publishers Limited
25 Eccleston Place, London SW1W 9NF
and Basingstoke

Associated companies throughout the world

Created by Working Partners Limited
London W12 7QY

ISBN 0 330 34910 4

1 3 5 7 9 8 6 4 2

A CIP catalogue record for this book is available from
the British Library.

Typeset in Bookman Old Style by SX Composing DTP, Rayleigh, Essex
Printed and bound in Great Britain by Mackays of Chatham plc, Kent

Chapter One

"And they're off!" the announcer cried, causing a large cheer to erupt from around the crowded stadium.

A pack of greyhounds raced down the straight, tightly bunched together in hot pursuit of the mechanical hare.

Spellbound, Neil Parker and his younger sister Emily watched as they rapidly approached the corner of the stand where they sat. Behind them, their parents, Bob and Carole Parker, watched too.

Bob and Carole ran King Street Kennels and Rescue Centre in the small northern country town of Compton. The whole Parker family was dog mad. They had come to watch a greyhound race meeting just outside Manchester because Emily's class at Meadowbank School was doing a project on how fast animals can run.

"Look at them go!" Neil shouted above the noise, peering into the distance as the greyhounds turned the bend and headed away from them again.

"Greyhounds reach speeds of around 50 kilometres an hour," Emily said, wisely. She pulled her thick woolly hat down over her hair and stamped her feet to help keep out the cold of the winter's night.

Neil shoved her playfully. His sister was always spouting animal facts. "So what's the fastest animal on earth, then?" he asked.

"A cheetah," Emily replied, "but I'm not sure how fast they go."

"Up to 95 kph, I think," said a voice from behind.

Neil turned round. His father was scratching his shaggy beard. "I saw something about them on TV recently."

The greyhounds were approaching the bend to the home straight, all still tightly bunched together. There was hardly anything between them. Suddenly, as they reached the last turn, there was a loud yelp. The crowd gasped as one

of the leading dogs stumbled and fell over, howling with pain.

Emily flinched and grabbed Neil's arm.

The other greyhounds ran around the injured dog and sprinted for the finish line. Behind them the stricken animal rolled over and then shakily stood up.

Neil looked round at his father. "That dog's hurt," he cried.

Bob nodded, keeping his eyes on the injured greyhound, all thoughts of following the winner gone.

The lame dog stood still for a moment. Then it hobbled after the disappearing pack, running as fast as it could but limping badly on its injured leg.

A murmur of sympathy rose from the crowd.

The dog hadn't reached the line by the time the commentator gave the race winner's name and the runners-up.

"And bringing up the rear is poor Flash Muldoon," the commentator finished. "Time for Flash to retire, perhaps?"

There was scattered applause as the dog crossed the finish line.

"Retire?" Emily asked. "Why? He doesn't look that old to me."

Carole Parker glanced at the race programme. "According to this he's two and a bit, Emily," she explained. "That's quite old for a racing greyhound."

"What happens to him now?" Neil wondered.

Bob's expression turned thoughtful. "With luck, he'll find a good home. There's an organization that specializes in homing retired greyhounds."

"But he looks lame," Neil pointed out.

Emily looked at Bob pleadingly. "Can't you do something, Dad?"

Bob frowned. "I'm sure there's a vet on duty who'll see to him, Emily."

"Besides," Carole added, "I'm sure Flash's owner will take care of him."

Neil and Emily looked at each other anxiously and then down at the track where Flash Muldoon was being led away. They hoped so.

As the Parkers drove back to Compton in the King Street Kennels Range Rover, Neil sat staring gloomily into the dark night.

Emily nudged him. "What's the matter with you? Didn't you have a good time?"

"Sure," Neil replied. "But I keep thinking about that lame greyhound. I wish I knew for certain that he's going to be OK."

"So do I," Emily agreed.

Neil peered at the race list he'd got with his entry ticket. "We've got his owner's name. We could ring him up and ask."

Carole sighed. "Honestly, Neil, the owner is probably a very responsible person. I doubt Flash will be out on the streets just yet. Anyway, we can't rescue every dog in the world, Neil. At least Flash has a home at the moment. There are hundreds of dogs who haven't."

Neil stared out of the window again. It was bitterly cold and the leaden night sky oozed a mixture of rain and snow. Suddenly he glimpsed a light-coloured bundle beside the road. As the

Range Rover passed it, the shape moved.

"Hey!" Neil cried. "That was an animal."

Emily jerked her head towards him. "Where?"

Carole, who was driving, had seen it too. She checked in her mirrors and then slowed down to a stop. "Hold on everybody." Looking over her shoulder, she slowly reversed up the dimly lit country road.

"It's probably a sheep," Bob said, peering into the bushes and ditches that bordered the road.

"There it is!" cried Neil moments later. It was much smaller than a sheep. He opened the back door and jumped out, just as the Range Rover rolled to a stop.

"Careful," Bob called out as Neil began to run towards the bundle. "If it's a fox, it might be vicious."

Neil's heart was thumping. If a car had hit the animal, it might be very badly injured.

Bob followed with a torch.

Neil approached the animal slowly; he didn't want to frighten it. Then he stopped dead. Gasping in disbelief, he recognized the brindled markings and familiar lean physique. It was Flash Muldoon, the greyhound who had limped home last.

How did the dog get here? They were deep in

the countryside, miles away from the racing stadium.

Bob shone the torch on the bundle of fur and cursed as he too recognized Flash, then saw that though the dog still wore its muzzle, his warm coat was missing.

Neil walked over to the shivering greyhound and held out his hand for Flash to sniff.

The dog whimpered and gazed at him with big, sad eyes. Neil felt the icy wind pierce his woolly jumper.

"There, there," Bob said as he knelt down beside the dog, his eyes running quickly over the greyhound's body to check for signs of bleeding. Very gently, he felt the dog's ribs and underside to make sure that Flash had no other injuries apart from his lame forepaw. The dog trembled at Bob's touch but did not struggle. Bob carefully removed the dog's muzzle, and Flash seemed to relax.

"He's terrified," Neil said.

Bob nodded tersely. "Go and get a blanket from the boot."

"I've already got one," Emily said, coming up behind him.

Emily handed the blanket to Bob, who wrapped it around the greyhound and then lifted him up. "We'll put him on the back seat between you both," he said. "He'll be more comfortable there."

Emily and Neil nodded.

"Is he OK, Dad?" Emily asked.

"Seems to be, apart from an injured forepaw," Bob replied. His voice was tight with anger.

Emily and Neil got in either side of the greyhound.

"There, boy," Neil told Flash. "You're safe now." The dog flinched as Neil reached out to pat him. Neil felt a rush of anger at whoever it was that had mistreated the dog. "This is a case for the RSPCA. Can we ring Terri McCall when we get home?"

Bob glanced at his watch. "It's a bit late, Neil. I'll talk to her tomorrow."

When they arrived home, Kate McGuire, the King Street kennel maid, came out to meet them. She had stayed on after work to babysit Sarah – Neil and Emily's five-year-old sister.

"You poor lad," she said to Flash, when she'd been told what had happened. The greyhound wagged his tail weakly. "We'll get you right, don't worry."

Kate watched the dog's limp as she led him towards a pen in the rescue centre. "It looks like he's broken his toe," she said, frowning.

Once Flash was inside, she gave him a pain-relief tablet with a little meaty dog food to disguise its bitter taste.

"Dad said we should wait until tomorrow to call Mike," said Emily. Mike Turner was King Street Kennels' vet and he was on call twenty-four hours a day.

Kate agreed. "Yes, he'll probably need to give Flash an anaesthetic, so his stomach will have to be empty."

Neil looked at Flash miserably pushing the food around the dish. "He looks so sad, I don't want to leave him."

"Nor do I," said Emily.

Bob Parker popped his head round the main rescue centre door. "Come on, you two. It's late. I need to lock up. And Flash needs some rest."

Reluctantly, Neil and Emily dragged themselves away from the sad-looking dog and went inside the house.

Mike Turner arrived just as the Parkers were finishing breakfast on Sunday morning. Bob took the vet to see Flash with Neil and Emily close behind – eager not to miss the vet's expert diagnosis. Sarah came along too.

Mike looked at the greyhound's forepaw and shook his head. "It *is* a broken toe," he confirmed, after gingerly touching the inflamed area.

"How can you tell?" Emily asked.

"The swelling, mainly. It's a very common injury in greyhounds."

"So will you put his paw in plaster?" Neil asked.

The vet hesitated. "No. I'm afraid I'll have to amputate the toe."

"What?" Emily gasped.

"It's the best treatment," Mike assured them. "It'll heal quickly."

"But he won't be able to race again," Neil

protested.

Mike smiled. "Of course he will. Plenty of greyhounds race after they lose a toe. But given Flash's age, he should probably be thinking of retiring now."

Bob glowered. "I'll have to get on to the owner and try to get him signed over to us."

Mike Turner gently picked up the greyhound. "This is an emergency, Bob. I have to treat him now."

Bob nodded his agreement.

Mike Turner carefully lifted Flash onto a cushion inside a large pet carrier. Flash whimpered in pain despite Mike's gentleness.

Neil accompanied the vet to his car and opened the back door for him.

"You'll be better soon," Neil consoled the frightened dog. He reached through the mesh and stroked Flash's head.

Mike gently clicked the car door shut. "You can collect him this afternoon."

Nobody said anything as the vet's car disappeared down the road that led to Compton.

"Don't worry, Flash will be OK," Emily comforted Sarah, seeing her worried frown.

Neil stuffed his hands in his pockets. "You can come for a walk with me and Sam, if you like."

"And with Jake?" Sarah asked eagerly. Sam, the Parkers' beloved Border collie, had recently become a father – and his young son Jake had come to live with them at King Street Kennels. Jake's mother was another Border collie called Delilah who lived on neighbouring Old Mill Farm.

Neil laughed. Sarah loved puppies. "Not this time. Jake is still too young to go for long walks. We can give him a run around in the exercise field when we get back, OK?"

Sarah agreed grudgingly, and they went to fetch Sam from his basket in the kitchen.

As soon as Sam saw Neil, his feathery black and white tail wagged wildly and he came running to his owner. Neil bent down and ruffled Sam's neck, clipped on his lead and then took the dog and Sarah out for a walk on the ridgeway – a stretch of high ground that ran high above King Street Kennels and Compton town.

It was a bitterly cold morning and even Sam seemed to feel the freezing icy wind. They turned for home after just ten minutes, but as they trudged, shivering, across the ridgeway, Sam stiffened, and stared intently into the distance.

As always, Neil was alert to his dog's every action. "What's going on, Sam?"

Sam's ears peaked as if he was listening to something very far away. Every muscle in the collie's body was tensed. Neil peered into the distance, but he could see nothing.

"Come on," Sarah urged him. "It's freezing."

"OK," Neil grinned and began to jog along the path.

Sam did not follow. Frowning, Neil stopped and whistled. Eventually Sam turned and ran towards Neil. There was a nervous edge to the dog's movements. The collie had sensed something far across the ridgeway that Neil, as a human, could not.

Chapter Two

When they got back to King Street Kennels, Neil settled Sam back in the cosy warmth of his basket next to Jake in the kitchen, then went to look for Emily.

He found her sitting at the computer in the kennels office working on her school project. Bob was talking on the phone nearby. When Emily saw Neil, she got up and, holding her finger to her lips, led him outside.

"Dad's on the phone to Harry Grey at Priorsfield Farm," she told him.

"What's going on?" Neil asked.

"Search me. Dad had only just finished speaking to Flash's owner when the phone rang again."

14

Neil raised one eyebrow suspiciously. "What did the owner say?"

Emily winced. "That Flash ran away."

"What? That's rubbish! Flash could hardly walk!"

"I know," Emily agreed grimly. "But Dad said the most important thing is to get Flash better and then get him a good home. At least he's been signed over to us, now."

Neil shook his head in disgust. "That man shouldn't get away with it!"

"Who shouldn't?" Sarah asked, her pigtails jiggling as she ran up to them.

Emily and Neil exchanged a glance. "We think Flash's owner abandoned him because he hurt his toe," Emily explained.

"Put him in jail!" Sarah suggested.

As Neil and Emily smiled their agreement, Bob joined them. "Emergency stations, everyone! Harry thinks there's a pup stuck in an old badger set up at the farm. He can't get it out, so he needs our help. Who's coming with me?"

"Me," Neil cried. "Are you coming, Em?"

Emily shook her head. "I've got to get my project finished. It's due in tomorrow."

Sarah jumped up. "Can I come?"

"OK," Bob said. "So long as you promise

not to get in the way."

Neil rolled his eyes. *Ha! Impossible!*

Harry Grey scratched his head as he explained the situation to the Parkers. "I've tried everything," he said. "The poor little mite's stuck inside. But there's something blocking the entrance and I can't get my hand in."

The badger set was beneath an oak tree at the edge of a sheep field. The farmer's weathered face, framed by thinning grey hair, was clearly distressed. "The ground's too hard to dig," he went on, "and I'm afraid of hurting it if I use anything too sharp."

Bob Parker kneeled down to have a closer look as Neil and Sarah peered over his shoulder.

"You're right about the ground, Harry. And it looks like the earth has collapsed around the entrance. Are you sure it's a pup inside?"

"That's what it sounded like. Tuff here heard it and barked." The farmer smiled at the brown, smooth-coated Jack Russell terrier by his side. "When I came over it was yelping, but I haven't heard anything for a while."

Bob stood up. "We'll have to get it out some-how. It won't last the night down there."

"But how?" asked Neil.

"We can't dig it out," stated the farmer. "If the earth is unstable we could cause more of the set to collapse."

Bob frowned thoughtfully. "Maybe we should ring Terri McCall and ask if she's got any ideas." The local RSPCA inspector was an expert in helping animals in need.

"Can't do any harm, I suppose," the farmer agreed.

As Bob and Harry set off back to the farm, Neil lay on the ground and listened. He put his ear to the set entrance and, sure enough, he heard a very faint whimpering coming from inside. He winced. The animal sounded in pain.

Beside him, Tuff heard the noise too and barked several times.

"Don't worry, boy," Neil soothed as he tried to squeeze his hand into the hole. "I'm . . . trying." But his hand was also too big.

Sarah was watching him intently. "Let me try," she said.

Neil looked at his little sister.

Tuff tilted his head to one side, questioningly.

"My hand's only little," she pointed out.

Neil stood up. "OK."

Sarah bent down and reached into the set.

Neil watched as her hand squirmed into the

gap. Then her arm disappeared. "Can you feel anything?" he asked, anxiously.

Sarah frowned. "There's something in the way," she said. "Something hard."

"Can you get it out?"

"I'll have a go!" She reached even further into the set and tugged. Then she tugged again. "It's really stuck!"

She struggled to get a grip on it.

"Try again, Sarah," Neil insisted.

Sarah did. This time, she didn't tug, she pulled slowly, grunting with effort. Neil watched, biting his lip.

A tube-shaped lump of soil slid gradually out of the tunnel as Sarah forced the blockage behind it towards her.

"There it is!" Triumphantly, Sarah held up a large bit of broken-off tree root. One end looked as if the puppy had been chewing at it.

Neil quickly stood up and shouted across to his dad and Harry Grey who were already at the far end of the field. "Hey! Dad! Come back! We've unblocked the hole!"

Tuff barked loudly and helped catch their attention.

Neil turned back and inspected the piece of root. A hungry pup would try to eat anything.

Sarah was already reaching into the set again. "I can feel the puppy!" she cried. "It's tickly!"

"Here, try one of these, Sarah." Neil handed her a dog biscuit which Sarah put just inside the set. A moment later, a little bundle of fur emerged, blinking nervously in the light. It was covered from head to feet with mud. Neil brushed the worst of it off from around its head and chest to reveal a dirty black and tan coat matted with dried earth. He could tell from the pup's teeth that it was very young; probably no more than seven or eight weeks old. It was also far too thin.

"Can I hold it?" Sarah begged.

Neil handed the trembling puppy to her. "Hello," she said.

Sarah held the puppy tightly to her chest. The dog squirmed and tried to lick Sarah's face. Sarah giggled. "What breed is he, Neil?"

Neil scratched his head thoughtfully. "I don't know. He looks a bit like some sort of mountain dog – his paws are quite big. I bet he's a cross of some sort. We'll have to wait until he's had a bath before we know for sure. I can't under-stand how he got here, though."

Sarah began to carry the puppy back towards the farmhouse. "Well, he's ours now."

Neil brushed himself down and watched Sarah show the puppy off to their dad. "I wonder if he was a Christmas present that somebody didn't want?" Neil mumbled to himself, as he followed her.

"Well done." Mike Turner beamed at Sarah and congratulated her as he examined the rescued puppy. The Parkers had taken the little dog to the surgery when they went to collect Flash. "You did brilliantly! This little fellow wouldn't have lasted much longer down there," Mike added. "You saved his life!" The vet expertly felt all over the pup's legs, head and tummy for any signs of injury.

Sarah grinned broadly.

"Will the puppy be OK?" Neil asked anxiously.

"I can't see any problems. He'll be as right as rain once he's had dinner and a good night's sleep," Mike assured him, peeking inside the puppy's mouth to look at his gums and teeth. "And a bath." Caked mud still covered some of the puppy's coat and paws.

"I'll help," Sarah offered happily.

"What are we going to call him?" Neil asked.

"Digger, of course," Sarah replied immediately. "Because he tried to dig his way out of that hole he got stuck in!"

Bob grinned and gently pulled Sarah's pigtails. "It's a good job we had you, Sarah."

Sarah beamed again, and stepped forward to cuddle the newly named puppy.

"I'll just get Flash for you," Mike said. He came back a moment later with the greyhound in tow. His right foreleg was wrapped in a heavy bandage. "Just keep the dressing clean and dry," Mike said. "You can change it in a couple of days."

Apart from his poorly leg, the greyhound was in peak condition. Flash looked graceful and strong with his long, sharp muzzle and appealing oval eyes.

"The stitches come out in ten days," Mike added. "Here are some pills to help with the residual pain. If there's a problem, give me a call. I'll look in on him next time I'm round."

"His owner should be prosecuted," Neil stated firmly.

The vet shook his head. "Your father says there are no witnesses."

"Yes, but he couldn't have just run away!" Neil objected.

"It's just possible," Mike said. "Even on three legs, Flash could still get away from someone, especially if they allowed him to."

Flash wagged his tail weakly as Neil took his lead from Mike. The greyhound sat quietly in his pet carrier in the back of the Range Rover for the journey home. Neil kept an eye on him to make sure he stayed still, while Sarah's attention was elsewhere.

Neil's sister looked very proud as she pushed her fingers through the smaller pet carrier nestled on her lap holding Digger.

"What's all the excitement?" Emily asked as she came into the storeroom between the two kennel blocks at King Street. Neil had already settled Flash in his pen and Bob and Sarah were running a bath for Digger.

"Sarah managed to get the puppy out of the badger set," Neil told her. "Harry and Dad were about to call the RSPCA!"

Emily grinned. "That's great! Top job, Sarah."

Digger emerged from his bath looking rather like a drowned rat, with his no longer fluffy fur slicked wetly to his body. Sarah helped Bob dry him with a hair dryer. He soon looked like a young puppy again. A white chest and muzzle punctuated his black and tan coat, and his ears flopped fetchingly over bright eyes. Digger positively preened as Bob carefully brushed his coat free of tangles.

"Digger's adorable, isn't he?" Sarah remarked proudly as she tickled the pup's neck.

"He's ideal for the website this week," said Emily. King Street Kennels had its own Internet website which Neil and Emily used to find homes for dogs in the rescue centre.

"Shouldn't we be thinking of Flash first?" asked Neil.

"We can't home Flash until he's recovered from his operation," Bob pointed out.

"OK," Neil agreed. "Digger it is, then. Let's

take his picture now!"

Emily picked up the puppy and affectionately touched her own nose against his. "Where shall we take it? Outside in the garden?"

Sarah frowned. "Digger's too tired," she said firmly. She gently cupped her hand underneath the dog and, taking him from her big sister, laid him gently against her shoulder. "You can take his picture tomorrow when he's had a sleep." The puppy yipped.

A car door slammed outside. Neil looked out and saw Sergeant Moorhead, one of the local policemen, going into the office. Leaving Digger with Sarah, who was happily fussing over him and brushing his fur, everyone else went over to see what was happening.

"I don't think so," Carole Parker was saying as they walked in the door. "Our dogs are never out alone."

"That's funny," Sergeant Moorhead said. "The woman said it sounded like a dog."

"What did?" Neil asked him.

The policeman folded his arms. "I've had a report of a strange animal on the ridgeway. A woman says her terrier was frightened half to death. I wondered if it was one of your dogs."

"Did the woman see this animal?" asked Bob.

Neil's mind was racing. He immediately thought about Sam's strange behaviour earlier.

"She only caught a glimpse of it in the early morning mist, but she heard it howl. She said it sounded like a wild animal!"

"It certainly wasn't one of our dogs," Bob assured him.

"I wonder what it was then," Sergeant Moorhead said. "The woman said it looked too big to be a fox. She thought it might be a wolf, but it couldn't be, could it, Bob?"

Before Bob could reply, Emily shook her head. "The only wolves in the country are in captivity. If one escaped, it would head for high, wooded ground. It wouldn't be happy on open ground like the ridgeway."

Bob raised his eyebrows. "What can I say, Sergeant? There you have it, from our resident wolf expert."

Emily blushed as the policeman grinned. "I thought so too, Emily, but that was what the lady said."

"Maybe she's imagining things," Neil suggested.

Sergeant Moorhead winked. "I hope so. I can't be doing with strange animals terrorizing Compton!"

Chapter Three

Neil woke up early on Monday morning looking forward to getting Digger's picture on the website before he had to go to school. A young puppy would attract lots of people to the rescue centre. One of the prospective owners might be interested in a toeless but lovable greyhound too.

At breakfast, Sarah had a thoughtful look on her face. "Jake's lonely," she said. "Why don't we keep Digger as a friend for him?"

Jake instinctively looked up from his basket where he was snuggled up cosily against his father's side and barked.

"No way!" Bob and Carole said together.

"Why not?" Sarah persisted.

"One puppy's enough," Carole said firmly. "Besides, you're not old enough to take care of a dog, Sarah."

Sarah scowled.

Neil finished his cereal and pushed his chair back across the stone floor noisily.

"Where are you off to?" asked Carole.

"I've just got time to get Digger's picture on the website, Mum. Is the Polaroid camera in the office?"

"Where it always is, Neil."

Emily followed Neil out and looked as puzzled as him when they discovered the cupboard in the office was empty.

"That's funny," Emily said. "Mum said it was here."

"Kate might have borrowed it," Neil suggested. "Maybe it's in the rescue centre."

The camera wasn't in the rescue centre either.

They found Sarah in Digger's pen. She'd given the puppy one of Jake's toys to play with. Digger was fascinated by it.

"Be careful," Neil warned her. "Puppies' teeth are very sharp. Don't leave him alone with it."

Sarah glared at him. "I know that, Neil."

Emily smiled at Digger, who was preparing to pounce on the squidgy blue ball. "It's awful, isn't it? Who could abandon a gorgeous little puppy like him?"

"Horrid people," muttered Sarah.

Neil shuddered at the image of the little animal being turfed out into the cold. "Come on, Em, it's time for school. We'll take that picture later. You too, Squirt."

Sarah's attention stayed on Digger. "I don't have to go yet. Mum'll call me when it's time."

Neil shrugged and left her to it.

"Have you heard about the Compton Beast?" Neil's friend Chris Wilson asked him. As they were in different classes, they had to sit in separate lines for assembly in the hall. But they

usually managed to end up near to each other.

"What are you on about?" Neil hissed. There was a no-talking rule, but Chris rarely paid attention to it.

"There's this thing that's been frightening people on the ridgeway," Chris told him.

"Oh, that. Sergeant Moorhead told us about it. The woman probably imagined it."

"*Kathy Jones* saw it as well," Chris emphasized.

Neil chuckled. "Yes, I thought she might have. Next she'll see the Abominable Snowman too." Kathy was notorious for telling tall stories.

"What d'you think it is?" Chris wondered.

Before Neil could answer, Hasheem Lindon, another of Neil's friends, chuckled. "Maybe Smiler's real self got out and he's been revealed as a vampire at last!"

Neil laughed at the thought of their head teacher Mr Hamley with fangs and a hooded black cloak.

Mr Hamley heard him as he was walking past to the front of the stage. "What's so funny, Neil Parker?" he demanded. "Maybe you'd like to share the joke with the rest of us."

"Er, um, there is no joke," Neil responded carefully.

"Then why are you laughing?"

Neil's nose wrinkled. There was no answer to a question like that.

On the way home from school, Neil stopped at the office of the *Compton News*. He just managed to catch the paper's photographer, Jake Fielding, who was on his way to a council meeting.

"I've got a story for you," Neil told Jake hopefully.

"Yeah? What's that?"

"We've rescued a racing greyhound called Flash Muldoon. He broke his toe in a race we saw in Manchester. Then he was abandoned in a ditch. He would have starved to death if we hadn't found him."

Jake Fielding nodded. "So it's a cruelty story. Is the owner being prosecuted?"

"Well, no," Neil replied. "He says Flash ran off, and there are no witnesses. Mike Turner says it's just possible that he could get away, even on three legs . . ."

"So what you want is for us to help you find a home for a racing greyhound who's lost a toe?"

"Yes. He'd make a great pet, Jake. He's got a brilliant nature."

Jake Fielding grinned. "As always, Neil. I'll see what I can do. But, to be honest, I've got other things on my mind. What I'd really like is a picture of the Compton Beast."

"Not you as well," Neil grumbled.

"What d'you mean by that?"

Neil stuffed his hands in his pockets. "I'm sure it's nothing, Jake. Either it's a large dog who's got away from his owner or it's a lost sheep or something. It hasn't actually attacked anyone."

"There've been three or four sightings so far. Seriously, Neil, that's the hot story this week. I'd sell my granny for a picture of the Beast, but I will try to take a picture of your greyhound."

Neil cycled back to King Street Kennels. When he got home, Jake pounded excitedly up to greet him. Neil affectionately ruffled the pup's coat, said hello to Sam, and grabbed Jake's lead to take him for a run in the exercise field. The puppy barked excitedly at the prospect of some fun.

On the way out, Neil stopped by the telephone to call Chris. "Kathy Jones," he began, when Chris answered, "where exactly did she see this so-called mystery animal?"

"Aha! I knew you'd believe it in the end! The ridgeway," Chris replied. "Are you going to have a look for it?"

"Of course not. I'm just interested, that's all."

"Yeah, right!"

"Well," Neil began, "Sam did, kind of, *sense* something up there yesterday. I suppose there might be an animal lurking about." Neil quickly wound up the conversation and headed outdoors.

As Neil passed through the yard with Jake, he saw Kate. The kennel maid looked harassed. "What's the matter?" he asked her.

Kate groaned. "The kennels are full and so is the rescue centre. We're rushed off our feet. Carole's doing the feeds and Bob's exercising the kennel dogs. I'm exercising the rescue dogs, but it'll take for ever . . ."

"Can I help?" Neil offered, as Jake tugged impatiently at his lead.

Kate smiled gratefully. "I thought you'd never ask! But you'd better take Jake for his walk first."

Neil headed for the exercise field. The puppy trotted along, sniffing everything. In the field, Neil let Jake off the lead and tried to teach him to "come" but the puppy treated everything as a huge game. When Neil gently pushed Jake's bottom down in a sitting position, the puppy rolled over completely and wouldn't get up again. Jake seemed very ticklish too, and squirmed and wriggled every time Neil tried to attach his lead to his collar. Twenty minutes had passed before Neil finally managed to get Jake under control and safely indoors.

Neil smiled to himself as he headed back to help Kate, who was walking Digger into the exercise field.

"What shall I do next?" Neil asked Kate.

The kennel maid struggled with Digger as he sniffed at a molehill. Digger seemed to like

exploring holes. "There's Flash," she said. "You need to put a boot over his bandage and then take him out to do his business. Don't forget to keep his bandage dry."

"OK," Neil said.

As everyone was finishing their dinner later that evening, Bob glanced at his watch. "Training class starts in half an hour," he said. "I've got a couple of new pupils." This week Bob's obedience classes had been moved from Wednesday to Monday, because the Compton Dramatic Society had announced that they wanted to hold some auditions.

"I'll bring Jake," Neil said.

"And I'm going to put Digger on the website," Emily added. "I got a lovely picture of him."

"You found the camera, then. Where was it?"

"In the laundry basket! Dad found it when he was doing the kennel bedding. I've no idea how it got there. Here, take a look."

Neil took the photo from her outstretched hand. It showed the puppy sitting in the garden with his head cocked to one side. Neil had to admit that Digger looked adorable.

"Who could resist him?" Emily asked.

"I don't know, Em. You have to housetrain a

puppy and then train it. There's always mess and there's often damage too. And they chew things when they're teething. Remember Jake ruined my new trainers?"

Emily laughed. "Yuck! I'm surprised he survived!"

Neil grunted.

"You should have hidden them!" Sarah said.

Bob's brow furrowed. "Talking of Digger, Mike Turner's sending some people over to see him tonight. Their dog died before Christmas, so they're looking for a new one."

Sarah's ears pricked up.

Emily grimaced. "That's a pity. Digger would have been a great advertisement for the rescue centre."

"Put him on the website anyway," Bob told her. "They might not be suitable."

Emily stood up.

"Can I help?" Sarah asked.

Emily and Neil exchanged a glance. Sarah wasn't exactly a computer whiz. "Of course you can," Emily said.

Carole began to load the dishwasher. "Only half an hour, Sarah," she said, "then you've got to get ready for bed."

*

As the training class began in Red's Barn, Neil heard the sound of a car stopping outside. Keeping hold of Jake's lead, he opened the barn door expecting to see another dog owner, but it was a middle-aged couple without a dog in sight.

"Hello," the man said. "I'm John Graham, and this is my wife Jan. Mike Turner said you have a puppy who needs a home?"

"I'll just get my father," Neil said. Instinctively, he liked the look of them already and hoped that they would think Digger would be a wonderful pet.

"I'll come and say hello, but would you show them round, Neil?" Bob said. "I can't leave the class and your Mum's up to her ears in paperwork. If they're interested, we'll arrange for them to come back."

Neil let his dad take over Jake's lead then took Mr and Mrs Graham over to the rescue centre. "Digger's only been with us a couple of days," Neil explained over the din of barking dogs as they crossed the courtyard. "We think he might have been an abandoned Christmas present."

Mrs Graham nodded knowingly. "We lost our dog two months ago, after fifteen years." Her face saddened. "We were heartbroken."

Neil couldn't commit himself without Bob's permission, but Mike wouldn't have sent the Grahams to King Street if he didn't know that the couple would make good, responsible dog owners.

"And here he is. Meet Digger," he said, as they reached the puppy's pen. The little dog was dozing, but soon sensed people outside and jumped up, wagging his tail.

"Aren't you sweet?" Mrs Graham said, holding her hand to the wire mesh. Digger sniffed her fingers happily. Neil opened the pen door after checking that all the other pens were shut.

Digger trotted out, wagging his tail so wildly that his whole body swayed. Mrs and Mrs Graham bent down to talk to him.

"What kind of dog is he, d'you know?" Mr Graham asked.

"We think he's got some mountain dog in him, but we can't be sure because we don't know his background."

"He'll be quite big, then?"

"About the size of a Labrador, I think."

"Our Honey was a golden retriever," Mrs Graham smiled.

As the barking died down, Neil noticed that

Flash was suspiciously silent. When he looked in the greyhound's pen, he saw that the dog was intent on chewing his bandage off.

"*No!*" Neil cried, as he quickly opened the pen and went inside. Flash wagged his tail guiltily. Putting the greyhound on his lead, Neil excused himself and then went over to the office. "D'you know where that plastic collar is?" he asked Emily. "Flash is chewing his bandage."

"It's on the shelf in the storeroom. I'll get it," Emily replied.

Sarah followed Neil back to the rescue centre. As he waited with Flash, she went over to the Grahams, who were playing happily with Digger. Flash glanced at Neil, and then began to gnaw at his bandage again.

"No! Stop it!" Neil urged.

Flash looked frustrated but he obeyed. Neil could hear Sarah talking to the Grahams. "My brother's got a puppy," she was saying earnestly. "You have to housetrain a puppy and then train it. There's always mess and there's often damage too. They chew things when they're teething."

"Sarah!" Neil hissed. She was repeating his conversation with Emily word for word.

Sarah ignored him. "And he ate his new trainers," she continued.

Neil peered out of the pen. The Grahams looked thoughtful.

"Sarah!" he called again. This time she came over.

"Yes?" she asked, innocently.

"Sarah, they've had a dog before. They know what a puppy's like."

"I was telling the truth," she protested. "Dad says it's important new owners know how dogs behave."

Neil frowned as Emily appeared with the big conical plastic collar that would prevent Flash chewing his bandage off. After they'd fitted it onto a distinctly subdued greyhound, Neil returned to the Grahams.

"He's such a lovely little dog," Mrs Graham said, smiling at her husband.

"If you'd like him," Neil said, "you'll have to talk to my father first."

Mrs Graham patted Digger one final time and then she stood up. "He's very sweet, but when we talked to your sister, we realized we might be better with an older dog."

"We've got a greyhound," Neil began.

Mr Graham shook his head. "Thank you," he

said firmly, "but we'd better think about it some more."

Mrs Graham smiled wistfully. "I just wonder if we might be better off with a cat."

Neil watched them leave, shaking his head. Sarah was obviously determined to make it very difficult to find a home for Digger.

"Don't you ever do that again," he told her.

"I told the truth!" Sarah insisted.

"You put them off *deliberately*, Squirt."

Sarah's lips puckered. She looked as if she was going to cry. "I don't want to lose Digger," she complained.

Neil sympathized with her. "Look, Sarah," he explained gently, "we can't keep every dog in the rescue centre."

"I know!" she replied. "But Digger's only little. He won't take up much room!"

Neil frowned. "But he'll grow *bigger*. We don't have room for him, not with Sam and Jake and the dogs in the rescue centre. It's kinder to find him a home of his own."

Sarah's head tilted to one side, but she said nothing.

"Isn't it?" Neil insisted.

"S'pose so," she agreed, reluctantly.

Chapter Four

"I've got a good idea," Sarah announced the next morning, at breakfast. "Why don't we house-train Digger ourselves? It'd be much easier to find a home for him, then."

"Oh, no," Carole said, shaking her head.

"It'd be easier to find a home for Digger if you didn't put people off," Neil told her.

"I was trying to help," Sarah protested innocently.

"I know," Bob said. "But next time leave it to us, eh, sweetheart?"

Sarah looked hurt. But then a moment later, she asked if she could take Digger for his morning walk.

"If Kate says it's OK and you keep him on the lead and stay in the exercise field," Bob replied. "You mustn't go out of sight."

Sarah's face brightened again.

"D'you fancy a Beast hunt?" Chris asked Neil, when school was over later that afternoon.

Neil grunted. "It still all sounds pretty far-fetched to me."

"Oi! You said Sam sensed something."

"He did, but it was probably another dog, not this Beast that people are talking about."

"It might be a puma," Chris suggested. "Like the Beast of Bodmin."

Neil shook his head vigorously.

"What do you think it is, then?"

"I don't know," Neil said.

"I was wondering, could it be some sort of wild dog?"

Neil frowned. "It's far too cold for a dog to be outside."

Chris got onto his bike. "We may as well have a look around."

"OK," Neil agreed.

When they got to King Street Kennels, the *Compton News* van was parked outside. Jake

Fielding was just coming out of the exercise field with Bob and Flash.

Neil and Chris ran over to meet the photographer. "Did you get a good picture of Flash Muldoon?" Neil asked him.

"Sure did," Jake grinned.

"So there'll be a story about Flash in the *Compton News*?" Neil asked hopefully.

"If there's space," Jake nodded. "The hot story of the moment is still the Beast, of course."

Neil groaned.

"I'm off to have a look for it now," he continued. "While it's still light enough. It was seen this morning on the other side of town." He held his finger to his mouth. "But keep it a secret, eh? I want to find it first!"

"Can we come?" Chris asked.

Jake Fielding looked at Bob, who shrugged in agreement. "As I was saying," Bob said, "I'm sure it's a wild-goose chase. A couple of the sightings might be a large dog who got away from its owner, but the rest of it's wishful thinking."

The photographer chuckled. "Where's your imagination, Bob?"

They all piled into the van together and Jake

started the engine and drove off. "I reckon the moors above Priorsfield Farm are our best bet," he said.

"Did Harry Grey see it?" Neil asked sceptically.

Jake Fielding shook his head. "The postman saw something this morning when he was doing his rounds."

Chris grinned gleefully. "This should be fun," he said.

The photographer parked the van about a mile outside Compton, high on the moors. "It was right here, the postman told me," he said, optimistically. He opened the back of the van and began to unload his equipment; a camera bag first and then a heavy tripod, which he hefted onto his shoulder. Finally he took out a video camera, which he asked Neil to carry.

"Why d'you need a video camera?" Neil asked him.

Jake chuckled. "Be prepared, that's my motto. If there is a Compton Beast, and if I got video tape footage as well as a picture of it, I could retire."

Neil and Chris gaped at him.

"If it's a real Beast," Jake said, "a picture

would be worth thousands of pounds; the video tape at least as much again. All the newspapers and TV stations would want it and they'd each have to pay to use it."

They began to walk over the moors. With every step that Jake Fielding took, the equipment clanked loudly.

"Any animal will be long gone way before we see it," Neil said. "You're a mobile sound effects unit, Jake."

"Can't be helped," the photographer replied philosophically. "I'd look pretty stupid if I saw the Beast and I didn't have the right equipment, wouldn't I?"

When they reached the flat expanse at the top of the moor, they stopped and looked around. Although sheep were scattered on the lower ground of Compton Vale, there was nothing else for miles around.

"Told you," Neil said.

Jake took a pair of binoculars from his bag and scanned the landscape. Neil blew into his hands; it was getting colder by the minute.

Jake then dropped the binoculars to peer into the distance before looking through them again. "There is something there," he said.

"What, a Yeti?" Neil joked.

The photographer handed him the binoculars. "See for yourself. It's about half a kilometre away, in that old sheep pen on that rise over there. It's dark-coloured, about the size of a large dog."

Neil looked. When he zoomed in on the square stone shape of the sheep pen he saw a dark object that moved slowly. Neil was astonished. "You're right, Jake!"

Chris had a look too. "Yes!" he cried. "Bingo! We did it! We found the Compton Beast!"

"Not so quick," Jake cut in. "We haven't got a picture yet." He frowned. "It's too far away, even with a telephoto lens."

"So what do we do?"

"Simple," Jake grinned. "You two go behind it. I'll follow and set up my equipment and you drive it towards me."

"If it is the Beast, it'll attack us!" Chris protested.

The photographer smiled. "There's no reports of it actually hurting anyone," he cajoled. "It startles people, that's all."

Neil was thinking. "It's not likely to attack us, Chris," he said. "It'll probably run away. Even if it's injured, it's not dangerous unless we corner it, and we won't." He turned and nodded at Jake. "Come on, Chris, it's not far away. If we run, we'll be there in no time."

Neil started off, with Chris following. As they jogged along, their breath made steamy trails in the freezing air.

There was a small dip between them and the sheep pen, so they couldn't see the animal until they got right up to it.

"I'm not so sure about this," Chris panted, as they drew closer, minutes later. Jake was about two hundred metres behind them, fixing a camera with a long lens to his tripod. When he saw they'd stopped he waved them on frantically.

The walls of the pen were crumbling but still about five feet high. Once they were directly behind it, Neil and Chris still couldn't see anything.

Neil steeled himself and crept silently right up to the stone wall. Holding his breath, he found a foothold and stepped up.

On the other side, inside the pen, he saw a large brown goat. It was munching determinedly at a clump of grass. Neil blinked. He knew the goat; it belonged to Harry Grey and it was always wandering off.

"What is it?" Chris asked anxiously.

Neil waved him over. "It's a goat!"

Jake made a sign to indicate he was ready.

Neil and Chris looked at each other. The goat was still munching. It completely ignored them.

Neil glared at Jake Fielding. His arms were waving wildly. "It's a goat!" Neil yelled.

The photographer cupped his hand to his ear.

"A goat!" Neil roared and then started laughing.

By the time they set off back to King Street, night had fallen. "Oh, well," Chris said from the back of the van. "At least we know what it isn't."

"We'll have to tell Harry Grey," Neil said.

Mist swirled around the moving vehicle and Jake Fielding clutched the steering wheel tightly. "The hunt goes on," he said, grimly. "D'you have any ideas?"

Neil shrugged. "It's like Dad says. It's mostly wishful thinking."

"I suppose a brown goat does look pretty beast-like from a distance," Chris pointed out.

Just then, the van's headlights lit a murky shape; for an instant, twin points of light shone brightly back at them and then they were gone.

"Stop!" Neil cried. "What was that?"

The van skidded to a halt, but by the time they got out, the animal was gone. They had no chance of finding it again in the misty night.

"What do you think it was?" Jake wondered.

"A fox?" Chris suggested.

Neil said nothing. The largest fox was about half-a-metre tall, and the eyes in the headlamps had been more than a metre above the ground.

The animal they'd seen couldn't have been a fox. But if it wasn't a fox, what was it?

Chapter Five

Neil sat in school assembly on Wednesday morning, shivering. The boiler wasn't working and it was freezing. Even Mr Hamley, standing behind a large wooden lectern at the front of the hall, was wearing his thick jacket as he spoke to the school.

It was very difficult for Neil to concentrate.

"This is cr-cruelty," Hasheem stuttered. "We should pr-protest."

Then the school secretary came into the hall and had a whispered conversation with the head teacher. A moment later Mr Hamley announced that school was closing early that day because of the unreliable heating system.

The hall emptied amidst scattered cheers.

Outside, Neil told Hasheem the story of yesterday's hunt. Emily listened, giggling.

"All we found was Harry Grey's goat," Neil admitted. "The old girl's always wandering off. Dad phoned him last night about it."

"And what did he have to say about the Compton Beast?" asked Hasheem.

"He thinks it's a wild dog. One that's been allowed to wander. One of his farmer mates said something had scattered his flock yesterday. So even Harry is keeping an eye out for it."

"So there is something?"

"I reckon so. Farmers round here are not going to put up with any nonsense while the sheep are in lamb."

Neil felt a flash of sympathy for the animal, whatever it was. He'd hoped it had the sense to keep away from fields full of sheep. But there wasn't much chance of that in Compton, which was surrounded by farms.

Hasheem laughed. "Nice story, Neil, but the mystery's solved," he told them. "It's one of those Eskimo dogs."

"What are you on—" asked Neil.

"You mean a husky?" Emily interrupted.

"That's it. Belongs to that weirdo George

Mullins. The pig farmer. He's got a smallholding on the edge of the moors."

Neil had seen the man around Compton, but he'd never spoken to him. He didn't seem very approachable. "Are you sure?" Neil asked. "Why didn't you tell me earlier?"

"Didn't have the chance. Anyway, my little sister and her friend saw him with it yesterday afternoon. Her friend saw the Beast on the ridgeway. She said it's definitely the husky."

"It makes sense, I suppose," Neil said grimly, thinking of the eyes that he'd seen last night. "Huskies have thick arctic coats. They're one of the few breeds of dog that could survive the freezing temperatures."

Emily shivered. "Let's get home before *we* freeze to death."

"No," Neil said. "I'm going to have a word with Mr Mullins. If his dog is the Beast, it's in danger if he doesn't keep it under control."

Mr Mullins' smallholding was about half a mile out of Compton on a winding country track. Neil got off his bike and looked around. The place seemed deserted. The L-shaped house was a little way off the road with a tidy yard in front.

"Hello?" Neil called. Nobody answered his

knock on the side door, but somewhere close inside the house a dog barked. The sound was deep; it was a large animal.

Neil walked slowly up to the door. If the dog was allowed to wander at will, it could be aggressive.

"Hello?" Neil called again through the letterbox. When nothing happened, he crept up to a window. Neil peered into the gloom.

Suddenly a large doggy face appeared at the window, snarling.

Neil stepped back, shocked.

The husky's dark tongue looked sinister as it lolled from its slobbering jaws.

"It's OK, boy," Neil told the dog softly.

The dog stopped snarling but a low growl came from its throat to warn Neil that he was on guard.

Neil turned to leave. Just then, the front door of the house swung open.

"What do you want?" A tall and sturdy man with thick white hair and beard stood in the doorway.

"Hello, Mr Mullins. I'm Neil Parker from King Street Kennels . . ."

"I don't care who you are! What are you doing skulking around my property?"

"I just wanted to . . ."

Mr Mullins raised his arm threateningly. "Away with you before I call the police!"

"Your dog might be in danger," Neil explained.

"Rubbish! No dog of mine is in danger. Now get off my land or I'll have the law on you." With that, George Mullins slammed the door in Neil's face.

"I was only trying to help," Neil protested, as he walked miserably away.

"You did your best," Emily consoled him later, as Neil sat in the kitchen drinking hot chocolate. "There's nothing you can do if he won't listen."

"You know what some farmers are like," Neil said. "If there's a dog worrying their sheep, they'll shoot it on sight. If Mr Mullins lets his dog wander, it's in terrible danger, even apart from the danger it's in of getting run over, or something like that."

"Hmmm," Emily mumbled. "I still can't see what we can do." Her gaze shifted to the window. In the courtyard Sarah was playing with Digger. "At least somebody's happy. Sarah's getting very attached to Digger," she added thoughtfully.

Neil frowned. "She's not neglecting Fudge?" Sarah's hamster usually meant the world to her.

"Of course not! She was just complaining that she can't play with him much during the day because he just wants to sleep." Emily got up. "I'd better get back to the computer. I was trying to find out something about wild dogs on the Internet."

"Anything interesting so far?" Neil asked.

"Not really. They're most common in urban areas, where they tend to form packs. Dogs are social animals, as we know, not loners. A wild dog on its own in the countryside would be highly unusual."

"So it's likely that Mr Mullins' husky is the Compton Beast," Neil said sadly.

"It looks that way," Emily agreed.

After Neil had exercised Sam and Jake in the field, he headed for the kennels office. Bob was on the phone, while Emily was at the computer. Listening intently to his conversation, she held her finger to her lips to tell Neil to keep quiet.

"Yes," Bob was saying, "I understand the problem, Harry. I'll ring Terri McCall right now." He listened for a moment, rubbing his forehead, then scratched his beard. "If you can't locate the owner, of course we'll take it in. But if it's vicious, we'll have to think again."

Neil's stomach tightened with dread. He went to ask his father what was happening but as soon as Bob finished the call, he dialled another number. "In a minute, Neil," he said. "I need to call Terri."

Emily joined Neil at the door. "One of Harry Grey's sheep has been found dead," she explained. "It'd been savaged. There's a wild dog on the loose and Dad's trying to get hold of it before somebody shoots it!"

Neil groaned, thinking of the husky he'd seen an hour ago. The dog was large but it didn't seem to be particularly vicious.

Bob joined them a moment later. "Terri's coming by later this afternoon," he said. "She's giving evidence in a cruelty case, so she can't come any sooner. Harry's going to ask Sergeant Moorhead to look into it too."

"I know what it is, I think," Neil confessed.

"Emily's already told me about the husky, Neil," Bob replied. "I tried to ring Mr Mullins to talk to him, but I've discovered he's not on the phone. I'll tell Terri about it."

Neil and Emily looked at each other.

"This is a serious business," Bob said, grimly. "I don't want either of you trying to track this animal down. It's aggressive, whatever it is. It's already killed a sheep. I don't want you two getting hurt as well."

As Neil and Emily went into the house, they heard a scurrying sound and then the living room door slammed shut. Neil opened it to find Sarah hiding behind the couch with Digger.

Neil shook his head. "You know it's against the rules to bring the rescue centre dogs in here, Squirt."

"It was only for a minute, Neil," Sarah wheedled. "Digger gets lonely in the rescue centre." The puppy wagged his tail hopefully.

Neil smiled. "He won't be lonely for much longer. But it'll be much more difficult for him to settle down in his new home if you bring him in here. I know you're trying to be kind, but it's better to leave him where he is."

Emily smiled. "How did she sneak past Kate? That's what's worrying me!"

Sarah reluctantly took Digger back to his pen.

"I'm worried about that poor husky," Emily said, watching her little sister drag herself outside. "If he did kill a sheep, he's in serious trouble."

"I know," Neil agreed. "It's not the dog's fault if his owner's stupid. The dog didn't strike me as dangerous, anyway. Large, yes, but Mr Mullins did seem to have him under control."

"He wasn't under control when he killed that sheep," Emily pointed out.

"But we don't even know if the dog's done anything wrong. What we can do, Em?"

Emily thought a moment. "We could warn Mr Mullins."

Neil thought too. "He wouldn't listen. He's not exactly the sociable type."

"It's worth a try, Neil."

"OK," Neil agreed. He owed it to the husky to give its owner another chance.

At the smallholding, George Mullins was in the pigsty. The door of the house was open and the husky was lying in the thin winter sun. When the dog saw Neil and Emily he came over to the gate and barked, but he made no move to attack them. A dog his size could easily have cleared the low wall that separated them.

"Mr Mullins," Neil called out. "Can we talk to you for a minute?"

Mr Mullins appeared from the pigsty. "You again," he snarled. "I told you, I'll call the law if you don't leave me alone."

Neil felt a surge of anxiety even though he knew Mr Mullins didn't have a phone. The man really didn't want them there.

The smallholder glared at them. "What do you want anyway?"

Neil took a deep breath. "A sheep's been killed on Priorsfield Farm," he said, "and there's a rumour going around that your dog did it."

"What?" Mr Mullins roared. "Who said that?"

"There's an animal on the loose and it looks like your husky," Neil told him.

"It wasn't my Tank, whatever it was," Mr Mullins raged. "I'll have the law on anyone who says it was!"

"We just wanted to warn you," Emily said.

"Aye, well, I'm warned. I'll go down to Compton right now and sort this nonsense out." Mr Mullins closed the door of the sty, opened the gate and whistled to the husky, who jumped into the Land Rover parked at the side of the house. He drove off so fast that the Land Rover sent up a shower of mud in a wide arc that drenched Neil and Emily.

They looked at each other as Emily wiped the mud from her face.

"Tank, hmmm," Neil said.

Emily whistled. "What a name for a dog."

As Neil and Emily cycled back through Compton, they saw Mr Mullins' Land Rover leaving Mike Turner's surgery, so they went in to see what was going on.

"What happened?" Neil asked Janice, the surgery nurse.

"I don't know. I was in the recovery room. I heard some shouting, then Mike took off. He just said he'll be back in time for evening surgery."

Neil frowned. Surgery didn't start for two hours.

"Let's go home," Emily suggested. "There's nothing else we can do now."

"Tank's the main suspect," Neil said, as they cycled back to King Street Kennels. "The animal we saw from Jake Fielding's van was big, and Tank's big."

"And his coat's so thick the cold wouldn't bother him."

"I don't think Harry Grey would insist on a dog being put down, not if Mr Mullins can prove that it's under control."

"Harry Grey wouldn't," Emily said, "but one of the other farmers might."

They exchanged a glance. There had been trouble before in Compton for a dog who'd been accused of worrying sheep. Although the dog was innocent, it had only narrowly avoided being shot.

Tank's future wasn't looking good.

Chapter Six

"Great," Neil cried, when he saw the RSPCA van parked outside the King Street Kennels office. "Maybe now we'll get somewhere."

Terri McCall came out of the office just as he and Emily were parking their bikes.

"How's things?" she asked, brightly.

"We're really worried about this Beast story," Emily told her. "We know a husky that fits its description, and it's getting really serious now – something has killed a sheep."

"I know," Terri said. "It's an odd story. It does sound like a large dog. Most of the stories, I'm sure, are exaggerated, but it does seem that there's something on the loose."

"You will find it, won't you?"

Terri McCall sighed. "I'll try, but we raided a dog-fighting ring last night. The paperwork will take the rest of the week. The so-called Beast of Compton will have to wait."

Neil sighed deeply.

"Sorry," Terri said, opening the van door. "The police will be keeping an eye out for it. If you find out anything, let me know."

"There's a risk one of the farmers will shoot it," Neil told her.

Terri winced. "I know. The problem is, if it is a dog that's gone wild, it won't be easy to track down. You need special equipment, night-vision binoculars – that sort of thing. You'd

have a much better chance of finding it in the dark. I'm going to have to get a specialist wildlife inspector to help. I concentrate on domestic animals – I haven't a clue how to do it myself."

"This husky, it's owned by a smallholder called George Mullins," Emily said.

"Yes, Bob told me," Terri replied. "Sergeant Moorhead's going to talk to him." She frowned. "The name rings a bell, though."

"What sort of bell?" Neil queried.

"I can't remember. It might be another Mullins. I just saw the name in a report a while ago. I'll check at the office and let you know."

"I hope Mr Mullins isn't mistreating Tank," Emily said after Terri left.

Neil put his hands in his pockets. "I wouldn't have thought so," he said.

Neil cycled back to Compton that evening to see Mike Turner. He reached the surgery just as the vet's car drew up.

For once, the vet glowered at him. "I've just had a not very enjoyable afternoon, thanks to you," he grumbled.

"What do you mean?" Neil's nose wrinkled as Mike took a set of pungent overalls out of his car boot.

"Your friend Mr Mullins insisted that I clear his dog's name. When I said that meant an autopsy, he told me to do that. I've just spent the last two hours at Priorsfield Farm cutting up a dead sheep. Fortunately, Harry Grey gave his permission, but doing an autopsy of a long-dead sheep isn't a pleasant business."

Neil smiled; he couldn't help it. "So what's the verdict?"

"I can't be certain until I get the pathology results, but I found all the signs of pasteurellosis. That's a type of pneumonia. In other words, the sheep died of natural causes."

"But Harry said it had been savaged."

"I think some foxes had a go at the corpse. The bite marks were typical of foxes."

"So Tank's in the clear?"

Mike looked puzzled.

"Tank is Mr Mullins's husky."

Mike grunted. "So far as the sheep's concerned, yes, but if he goes barging around the place the way his owner does, he's liable to get into trouble. That man's a menace."

"I don't know what to do next," Neil said, gloomily. The Parker family had finished dinner. Emily was helping Bob stack the dishwasher while Carole got Sarah ready for bed.

"Maybe the fuss will die down," Emily said, hopefully. "Now we know the sheep died of natural causes, there's no proof that the so-called Compton Beast is a killer."

"Oh, well," Emily sighed. "The good news is that I got Digger on the website. When he's gone, we can concentrate on Flash."

"There should be a story about him in the Compton News tomorrow," Neil said. "Let's hope a greyhound-lover out there sees it."

"Unless Jake Fielding gets his scoop after all," Emily giggled.

Neil yawned. It had been a long day. He watched television with Emily for a while, and then he went to bed.

He lay awake thinking. What Emily said was right; there wasn't much more they could do about the Compton Beast.

Unless they managed to find it themselves.

In the small hours Neil was woken by the piercing screech of a siren. A moment passed before he realized that the kennel alarms had gone off. Through his curtains he could see that the emergency lights were lit.

He got out of his bed and ran to the window, where he saw Bob running over to the kennels. Neil rubbed his eyes and went downstairs.

The whole family had been woken up.

"What's going on?" Neil asked.

"Dad's gone to find out," Emily told him.

Neil looked outside again and saw his father checking the doors of the kennel blocks and then the perimeter fence. Bob went round the yard twice and then he came in again.

Just then, Sarah appeared. "Is Digger OK?" she asked, anxiously.

"Digger's just fine," Bob smiled, as he bent down to give her a hug.

Carole picked her up and whisked her back to bed.

"What was it, Dad?" Neil asked.

"I don't know. I couldn't see anything and all the doors are secure. The alarm's very sensitive. There's quite a gale blowing outside – it could be the wind that set it off."

"Or," said Emily falteringly, "it could have been the Compton Beast . . ."

Neil tutted then went back to bed. False alarm.

*

67

When Neil woke up again it was morning. The wind had died down and the sun was shining through the curtains. He hurriedly put on his school clothes and then went downstairs.

The mid-week edition of the *Compton News* was on the kitchen table. The headline declared *COMPTON BEAST – MORE SIGHTINGS*. Below the banner was a picture of Sergeant Moorhead with the caption: *Police investigate*.

Neil groaned. The story filled the entire front page and ran on to the second and third. The newspaper was running a competition offering a reward for a picture of the poor animal.

Flash had been relegated to a couple of inches at the bottom of the letters page. They hadn't even used the photograph.

"This is incredibly irresponsible," Bob said, glaring at the paper. "They'll cause panic with all this nonsense. Nobody's been hurt, the sheep died of natural causes. They're demonizing some poor animal for no reason. The next thing'll be that there's a posse out hunting for it!"

"You've got to see it from their point of view," Carole said calmly.

"They're creating mass hysteria!"

"I know," Carole continued. "But the whole town's been talking of nothing else all week.

They asked me about it in the supermarket in Padsham yesterday."

"Can I give Digger his breakfast?" Sarah piped up. "He must be very hungry."

"Yes," Carole replied, distractedly. "If Emily will take you."

"I can go on my own."

"You might leave the door unlocked. We can't risk any of the dogs getting out." Carole gave Emily a sharp look, and Emily took the hint.

"It's OK, Squirt," said Emily. "I want to see Digger too."

Sarah grinned, and led her big sister out towards the rescue centre.

"That competition's a con, Dad," Neil said. "Jake Fielding told me that a picture of the Beast, I mean, the real beast, if there is one, would be worth thousands of pounds."

Bob grunted. The phone rang and he got up to answer it. He said "no" a couple of times and then he put it down, shaking his head. "That was a farmer from Colshaw wanting to know if his sheep are in danger," he said. "Thinks I'm an expert on wild dogs. Huh! I suppose tomorrow there'll be a Colshaw Beast too!"

Neil went to give Sam and Jake their morning walks. As he came back, Emily beckoned him to the path that led away from the kennels towards the ridgeway. She was pointing to something in the frosty grass.

Neil saw a series of large paw prints. Jake sniffed at them inquisitively. The indentations of the pads were more than two centimetres across; the whole paw was six or seven centimetres wide. "It's a large dog, I think. It's bigger than any we've got in the kennels."

Emily went to fetch Bob. He studied the print closely for a minute. There were two distinct sets of tracks, one that led towards the storeroom and another that led away from it. The tracks vanished on the paving of the yard.

"Right, that's it," he said. "I don't want either of you going onto the ridgeway. Something's out there, and I don't want you getting hurt."

"But, Dad!" Emily protested.

"Dogs aren't normally vicious," Neil added.

"This isn't a normal dog," Bob retorted. "If it's been living in the wild it will revert to instinct. I'm not going to take any chances, and you're not going to either."

Neil looked at Emily. They both knew that it was pointless to argue with their father when he was in this sort of mood.

*

At school, everybody was talking about the Compton Beast. Neil listened glumly. The worst thing was that the boiler had been fixed. He'd been hoping for another day off.

"Kathy Jones has complained to the police about that husky," Hasheem told him at lunchtime.

"What?" Neil responded, horrified.

"People are saying it's vicious and it should be put down."

Neil groaned. "There's no proof that Tank's hurt anyone."

"I know, but they're saying that man Mullins doesn't keep it under control."

"That's not fair," Neil protested. "Tank hasn't done anything. It's just because they've decided he must be this mythical beast that people are talking about."

Hasheem shrugged.

Neil's gloom deepened. No one seemed to be interested in the truth. Tank's time was running out.

When school ended, Chris asked Neil if he was going back to King Street Kennels, but Neil shook his head. "I've got something to do first," he said. "You wouldn't know where I could get a pair of night-vision binoculars, do you?"

"The only person I know who's got them is Smiler," Chris replied. "He uses them for badger-watching. He gave a talk about it once."

"I wonder if he'd lend them to me?"

"I doubt it. They're his prize possession."

"Y'see, if we're going to track down the beast, we need the right gear."

"I'll ask him, if you like," Chris offered. "Nothing ventured, nothing gained." He laughed and rode off towards home.

Neil got onto his bike and cycled to Mr Mullins' smallholding.

Terri McCall had recognized the small-holder's name. That meant that he might have been accused of cruelty in the past. Neil hated to think of any dog being mistreated, and although it didn't seem like Tank was an unhappy dog, he was still very worried about the husky's safety.

He wanted to make sure Mr Mullins was taking care of the dog properly. If not, then Tank could be taken away from him and found a new home. The husky would be safe, and all this nonsense about the Compton Beast would die down. It was a long shot, but Neil decided it was worth a try.

Neil left his bike in a ditch when he neared the smallholding, which he approached on foot. He didn't want to attract Tank's attention so he found a vantage point behind a stone dyke about fifty metres away.

Neil settled down to watch. A plume of smoke rose from the chimney of the farmhouse, which surely meant that Mr Mullins was indoors.

Fifteen minutes passed and nothing happened, so Neil crept along the road and into the yard, where he hid behind an old plough. Tank's deep bark erupted from the house and Mr Mullins came to the window to look out.

Neil froze. After a moment, Mr Mullins talked to the dog softly and the barking stopped. Very slowly, Neil crept closer to the house, until he reached the window. A warning growl came from the other side. His heart thudding, he eased up and peered in.

Inside the room, Mr Mullins and Tank were playing a game of tug-of-war with a long plastic bone. The farmer was having a hard job hanging on to his end but the dog was loving it. Tank was dancing around on his hind legs, trying to box Mr Mullins' hands off the toy. They tugged back and forth for a while until Tank

lunged, knocking Mr Mullins over.

Laughing, Mr Mullins got up, ruffling the dog's shaggy coat. Tank picked up the toy again and held it hopefully for another game. Mr Mullins said, "Let's go for a walk."

Neil reacted immediately and scampered back across the yard, leaping over the wall just as the door opened. Tank headed straight for him, but his owner called him to heel and they headed for the hills.

Neil shook his head as he got onto his bike. "So much for that," he said to himself.

When he got back to King Street Kennels, he

phoned Terri McCall to tell her what he'd discovered.

"It wasn't a cruelty case I remembered, actually," she told him. "At least it wasn't Mr Mullins. He discovered a dodgy puppy farm on the other side of Padsham. He reported them to us and gave evidence when we prosecuted the owners. Tank was a puppy that he rescued himself. He's definitely a responsible dog owner."

"I just thought finding out a bit more about Mr Mullins might have been a way of helping Tank," Neil said.

"I don't think Tank's the dog that's causing the trouble," Terri replied.

"I know that, you know that, but some people have complained to the police about him."

"Oh, dear," Terri said. She thought about it for a moment. "It won't come to anything unless Tank does something," she continued. "I'm sure Mr Mullins has him well-trained." She chuckled. "He's one of these people who get on better with dogs than with humans. I'm sure Tank's safe with him."

Neil put the phone down. Tank might be safe with Mr Mullins, but whether the husky was safe in Compton was another matter.

Chapter Seven

"**G**reat news!" Emily said, as Neil went into the kitchen. "The boiler's broken down again, so there's no school tomorrow. It's been on the radio."

"Uh-huh," Neil mumbled. He was thinking about Tank.

"And a man in Compton asked me about Flash this afternoon," Carole told Neil. "He's living at the Grange now, but he used to own greyhounds. He said he'd love to come and see him. He'd spotted that little bit in the paper. I told him to come tomorrow."

Neil's frown deepened. King Street Kennels had already given one dog to the old people's home, a beautiful rough collie called Skye, so he doubted if there would be a place for Flash there too.

The phone rang. Neil answered it.

"I just thought I'd grab the bull by the horns," Chris said brightly. "So I asked Mr Hamley if we could borrow his binoculars."

"What did he say?"

"Do you really need to ask, Neil?"

"No," Neil replied grimly.

"Hey – d'you think if we took a picture of Tank and sent it to the *Compton News*, we'd get the money?" Chris went on.

"No," Neil said again.

When Carole was ready to serve dinner, Sarah had not appeared so Neil went to find her.

His little sister was in the rescue centre cuddling Digger. "Come on, Squirt," he said. "Dinner time."

"Dad says some people are coming to see Digger tomorrow," Sarah said, sadly.

"Well, that's good, isn't it? We want to make sure he's got a good home."

Sarah shook her head, her pigtails swinging from side to side. "Digger will miss us."

"Course he won't," Neil told her. "Puppies have short memories."

"But won't he remember that I saved his life?"

"I'm sure he will," Neil assured her.

Bob looked exasperated as the Parkers sat down to eat. "I've just had a call from a TV station in Manchester," he said tersely. "They're coming to interview me after dinner."

Emily was intrigued. "Why?"

"Because of all this nonsense about the so-called Compton Beast, of course. They want to do a story about it too."

"You don't have to talk to them," Carole pointed out.

Bob rubbed his neck. "I may as well. I might be able to put a stop to all this nonsense once and for all."

The TV crew arrived just as the Parkers had finished dinner. They all gathered around to watch as the cameraman set up his equipment in the courtyard in front of Kennel Block One and the reporter began to interview Bob.

"It does seem that there's some sort of animal on the loose," Bob agreed reluctantly.

"What sort of animal?" the reporter persisted.

"Possibly a dog, but obviously it's got to have a pretty thick coat, because of the weather. It's certainly not this *Beast* that people are talking about."

"The local people are frightened," the reporter continued. "Are they in any danger?"

"None at all, so long as they don't frighten the animal, or attempt to corner it," Bob said. "The RSPCA and the police are trying to find it. As soon as they do, all this fuss will be over."

Emily and Neil exchanged glances. "Don't hold your breath," Emily whispered.

As the crew packed up their gear, Sarah asked if her dad would be on television.

"It should be on the breakfast news tomorrow," the reporter told her.

Sarah clapped her hands together. "Goody! We'll be famous."

On Friday morning, Neil and Emily watched the local news bulletin with their parents. Bob was furious at the way the programme had dramatized the story. "Yet more scaremongering," he said, in disgust. "They've not used everything that I said. They missed out the bits where I said crowds of people going to look for it would do more harm than good."

Before the broadcast ended, the phone rang. When Bob answered, Mr Mullins shouted at him so loudly that the whole family heard what he said. "That animal's not my Tank," he raged. "I'll have you in court if you say he is!" The pig farmer hung up before Bob could protest.

Everybody was quiet for a moment.

But the silence didn't last long. Outside, everybody could suddenly hear the sound of heavy traffic. It was an unusual event in the normally very quiet country lane where they lived.

Neil looked outside and saw people heading for the ridgeway.

Over his shoulder, Bob was shaking his head

as he watched the crowds. "The power of television," he said, grimly. "The whole of the north of England is looking for the Compton Beast now!"

"They've got about as much chance of finding it as Jake Fielding has," Neil pointed out.

The Parkers ate breakfast in silence. After they finished, there was a knock on the door.

Emily opened it to see a couple with two young children. "Hello," the woman said. "We're the Thompsons – we've come to see the puppy who needs a home."

Sarah jumped up. "I'll take you!"

Bob stood up too. "No, Sarah, I will."

Sarah ran out of the kitchen up to her room.

Neil found her moments later lying on her bed, sobbing her heart out.

"It's not fair," she wailed. "I don't want Digger to go, and he doesn't want to leave me!"

"Digger needs a home," Neil tried to explain. "You wouldn't want him to stay in the rescue centre for ever, would you?"

Sarah didn't reply.

"When Digger has a home, he'll be happy," Neil reasoned.

"You said he'd remember me because I saved his life," Sarah murmured tearfully.

"I suppose he will," Neil agreed, "but he'll soon start enjoying his new life."

"Digger might. I won't," Sarah sobbed. "I'll miss him horribly and so will Fudge!"

"Come on," Neil suggested. "You help me take Jake for his morning walk."

Sarah went with him, but she didn't say a word. When they got back afterwards, the family had left.

"Did they take Digger?" Neil asked his father.

"No," Bob replied. "They're going to think about it and let me know. They like him very much, but they want to be sure that he's the right dog for them."

For the first time that morning, Sarah smiled.

Mr Gilmour from the Grange arrived a short time later to see Flash, after he'd phoned first to check that it was OK. He was a friendly old man whose eyes twinkled with fun, despite his bad arthritis which meant he needed to walk with the aid of a stick. Neil liked him instantly.

"I just wanted to see Flash," Mr Gilmour said, as Neil took him to the rescue centre. "I still follow the dogs, you see, and his great-great-grandfather was a dog of mine. Best dog I ever had. Won nearly every race he entered during his career, And afterwards he became our pet. My wife doted on him."

"Wow! You know his family!" Neil exclaimed. "That's incredible!"

Flash stood up in his pen and whimpered as he sensed a new friend. Neil opened the door and then Mr Gilmour bent down stiffly to talk to the dog. "You can see the blood line," he said to Neil as he patted the greyhound's flanks. "Flash has the same colouring and the same strong muscles in his hind legs."

Flash stepped carefully out of the pen; his paw hadn't healed completely yet but he was able to put his weight on it. "It's time for his morning walk," Neil said to Mr Gilmour. "You can come with us if you like."

The old man agreed as he straightened up. "I wish I could take him, Neil, but we've already got one dog at the Grange."

Flash picked up something from the floor and then nudged Mr Gilmour's hand. The old man looked down and saw that the greyhound was holding a sock.

"I have no idea where he found that!" Neil said.

Mr Gilmour took it and laughed. "His

ancestor Max was just like that. He fetched and carried like a Labrador, so he did."

Neil smiled.

"Racing's a different world today," Mr Gilmour went on. "Some of the trainers only care about winning, they don't care for the dogs at all."

"We saw that," Neil said. He told Mr Gilmour how they'd found Flash. The old man shook his head angrily.

Once they'd walked Flash round the field twice, they took him back to his pen. The greyhound's eyes followed them sadly as they closed the door.

"Best pets in the world, greyhounds," Mr Gilmour said. "They only need a couple of short walks a day and not much food. They're a healthy breed, so you shouldn't be bothered with vet's bills, the way you can be with these fancy show breeds."

He bent down to say goodbye to Flash through the wires of the pen.

But as they began to walk away, Flash barked.

Mr Gilmour and Neil went back over to him. The sleek, sparkly-eyed greyhound was holding Mr Gilmour's wallet in his mouth. The old man must have dropped it when he had been inside the pen.

"And intelligent too. See what I mean?" he said. "I wouldn't have got far without my money, Flash!"

Neil laughed as the greyhound wagged his tail happily.

"He'd make a great pet for someone like me," Mr Gilmour remarked, as they went outside. "I'm always dropping things. He's got the right instincts. He only needs a little bit of training and he'd be ideal."

"Do you think . . .?" Neil began hopefully.

"Once Flash's toe is heeled, we could have a go at training him together, if you like," the old man said smiling, as he guessed what Neil was going to ask.

"That'd be brill!" Neil said happily.

Mr Gilmour insisted on making a donation towards Flash's upkeep and then he left. "I'm sad to leave him," he told Neil, "but you'll take good care of him, I can see that."

"You bet I will." Neil waved goodbye thoughtfully. If only Flash could find a new home with someone like that.

The ridgeway was still thronging with people. Neil watched for a while and then he decided to go to Compton police station before he called on Chris. Sergeant Moorhead was inside, drinking his morning coffee. When the policeman saw Neil, his normally calm manner became edgy.

Neil grinned hopefully. "You're not paying any attention to these people who are complaining about Mr Mullins' dog, are you?"

The policeman frowned at him. "What business is it of yours, Neil Parker?"

Neil plunged his hands into his pockets. "It's unfair, Sergeant Moorhead. Tank's not aggressive. It's just because he's a big dog that people think the worst of him."

"The fact is, Neil, I've had a report that Tank was loose on the ridgeway the other day. There were some children there and the dog terrified them."

"But Tank didn't attack them, did he?" Neil quickly pointed out.

"No, but a dog that size shouldn't be out unaccompanied. No dog should. I've given Mr Mullins a warning, but he wouldn't listen. He denied it was him." The policeman was adamant. "We can't have a dog that size going around frightening people, Neil. It's got to be kept under control or there'll be trouble."

Neil thought hard as he cycled to Chris's house. The story didn't match what he knew about Tank and his owner, bad-tempered though Mr Mullins certainly was.

But something had frightened people. They couldn't all have imagined it. Or could they?

Tank's future was looking worse by the hour.

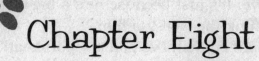

Chapter Eight

"We've got to be scientific about this," Chris said.

Neil and Chris were sitting at a large desk in his bedroom. An Ordnance Survey map of Compton was spread out on top of it. He'd marked all the sightings of the beast with red pencil. There was a whole cluster of marks around the ridgeway and scattered dots over the rest of Compton Vale.

"We can discount these ones," Neil said, pointing to the moors where they'd found Harry Grey's wandering goat.

Chris nodded. "It's got to be somewhere near the ridgeway, Neil. Most of the sightings are still around there."

"I know. I'm sure it set off the alarms the other night at our place. Dad got really spooked out by some huge footprints we found."

"Let's go, then," Chris said, standing up.

"Wait up! The ridgeway's full of gawkers. Besides, Dad told Emily and me to stay clear of it."

"That's never stopped you before!"

Neil ran his hands through his hair. "It might have moved on by now. The crowds could have frightened it off."

"So let's go over the moors and skirt the ridgeway," Chris suggested. "That way you're doing nothing wrong."

"OK," Neil agreed. They'd no better ideas anyway.

"What d'you reckon about this story that Tank frightened some children?" asked Chris.

"It just doesn't make sense. Tank's always with Mr Mullins, so it couldn't have been Tank on the ridgeway."

"It must have been," Chris reasoned. "There aren't two huskies in Compton, are there?"

"No," Neil said. "At least, if there are, I've never seen the second one."

"The mystery deepens," Chris remarked, wrinkling his nose.

On the way up to the moors, Chris and Neil

stopped to talk to Emily and Julie, who were standing outside the pet shop in the High Street. Julie was holding some leaflets.

"What are you doing?" Neil asked her.

He read the leaflet Julie handed him:

The so-called Compton Beast is not a beast but an animal which might be in danger. If you see this animal, please do not approach it. Report what you've seen to the RSPCA or send an e-mail to puppypatrol@ksk.co.uk

"It was Emily's idea," said Julie.

Emily shrugged. "I ran it off on the computer this morning. We couldn't think what else we could do."

Neil stuck his hands in his pockets. "We're going up to the moors to have a look round."

"Why don't you put out some food for it?" Emily suggested. "You can check tomorrow and see if it has been eaten. Something else might eat it first, but it still might give us a better idea of what's moving around up there."

"That's a great idea, Em," Neil exclaimed, and then his face fell. "But I don't have any money to buy some," he added. "And we might get caught if we took some from the storeroom.

Kate's just done a stock check."

Julie reached into her jacket pocket and handed him her weekly pocket money in coins. "There you are."

Neil grinned. "Thanks," he said. "We'll use Sam's old bowl."

Once they'd collected the bowl from King Street Kennels, Neil and Chris cycled along the road with Sam running alongside them until they had reached the far side of the ridgeway.

"This is as good a place as any," Chris said, as they left their bikes where the path joined the road and started off over the frozen ground. Even at this distance, they could see the people up on the paths that criss-crossed the surrounding hills.

"It's ridiculous," Neil complained. He held tight onto Sam's lead as they walked across the frozen ground. He didn't want Sam running off and being accused of being the Compton Beast!

"It was this morning's TV report that did it."

"I know. Dad's furious about it."

They walked deeper into the moors. As the ground rose there was scattered mist and drifts of snow that had not melted from the bad weather weeks earlier. Neil scoured the ground for paw prints but there were none. Sam sniffed the icy grass but was finding it difficult to smell anything interesting.

"This is pointless," Chris said. "The beast is long gone, whatever it is."

Neil scanned the landscape. He was looking for shelter, an old sheep pen maybe, or even a stone dyke that would act as a windbreak.

A long way away, Neil spotted a shape in the frosty air which he thought looked promising. The ridgeway was now a mile or so to the north of them. When Sam had noticed something before, he had looked due south – exactly in the direction of the structure Neil had just seen.

Neil crouched down beside Sam, put his face close to his and pointed towards the structure. "Can you feel anything, boy? Is there something there?"

Chris was paying close attention. He knew better than to doubt the razor-sharp senses of a dog.

Sam barked once and strained against Neil's arms as if he wanted to be released.

"Come on," Neil cried, as he broke into a run. "Sam thinks that's the place!"

As Neil drew closer to the object, he realized that it was an ancient mile-marker. The old road over the moors had passed this way. He stopped, out of breath. There was no shelter there.

"So where do we put the food?" Chris asked.

Neil looked around. On the next rise he could see something that looked bigger, an old barn or a ruined cottage maybe. But there wasn't time to get there and back home before night fell. If Bob Parker had to launch a search for Neil, that would be the end of Neil's hunt for the so-called Beast of Compton.

"Here's as good a place as any," Neil replied. Once he'd spooned the food into the bowl he left it at the foot of the stone.

"If you're out there, Beast, dinner's ready," Chris roared.

Sam barked again, responding to Chris's burst of energy.

"We'll check and see if it's eaten tomorrow," Neil grumbled. "But I don't hold out much hope."

"How did you get on?" Neil asked Emily later that night, as the Parkers ate dinner together.

"We handed all the leaflets out, but I don't

know if anyone will pay any attention to them."

"It's unfair that Tank's getting the blame," Neil complained. "I'm sure it wasn't him who frightened the children."

Bob grunted. "His owner's not helping matters, Neil."

Neil and Emily exchanged a glance. "It's not the dog's fault," Emily pointed out.

"It never is, Emily, but Mr Mullins really should know better than to go around the place shooting his mouth off," Bob reasoned.

"Maybe you should start classes to teach dog owners how to behave as well as their pets," Neil grinned.

"I can't work miracles, Neil." Bob laughed. "But the good news is that the people who came today have offered Digger a home. I think they'll be ideal for him."

Sarah dropped her fork.

"They're coming to collect him tomorrow afternoon," Bob said.

"I don't feel well, Mummy," Sarah moaned.

Carole looked at her. "You do look a bit peaky, Sarah. Perhaps you'd better go to bed early."

Sarah nodded meekly.

*

"I had a word with Matron," Mr Gilmour said, when he phoned Neil from The Grange Retirement Home on Saturday morning. "I told her that Flash was the great-great-grandson of my best dog, and she suggested that you bring him down to see us sometime. D'you think you could manage that?"

"I don't see why not," Neil replied. "I'll have to get Mum or Dad to bring him in the car, because he's still got his bandage on and he can't walk all that way. Anyway, I'm not sure Dad would want me walking him across the ridgeway."

"I'll come to collect you, if you like," Mr Gilmour suggested.

"OK," Neil agreed.

"I was thinking," Mr Gilmour went on, "I'd love to give Flash a home, and if we could train him to fetch and carry a bit, that'd help. Some of the old folk are always dropping things and losing things and if Matron saw that Flash could help, she might just go along with it. I'm sure Flash would get on well with Skye and he'd be a great pet for all of us."

Neil's hopes surged. "That's a brilliant idea."

The old man chuckled. "So if I come over this afternoon, we can start a bit of simple training."

As Neil was walking back to the kitchen, he remembered that Chris was coming round that afternoon.

"That sounds hopeful," Emily said, when Neil told her that the greyhound had made a friend.

"Yes," Neil replied in a whisper. "But Chris and I left that food out for the animal. I wanted to go and see whether it had been eaten."

"Ring Chris and tell him to come a bit later," Emily suggested. "If it stays as cold as it is, you might be able to follow its tracks in the frost."

Just then, the kitchen door opened and Carole Parker stepped into the warmth, blowing into her hands.

"Hi, Mum," chorused Neil and Emily.

Carole looked confused about something. "Neil? Did you borrow some of the rescue centre puppy food for Jake?"

Neil shook his head vigorously. "No. He's got plenty of his own. Look." Neil pointed to a stack of tins piled high on one of the kitchen shelves on the wall.

"Oh. It's just that some tins are missing. I've just found the storeroom door swinging open but I could have sworn I locked it this morning."

"That's strange," said Emily.

"It wasn't us," Neil assured her.

Carole looked around suspiciously.

"Maybe it was Dad," Neil suggested.

Carole shook her head. "Bob wouldn't have forgotten. It might have been me. I think the phone rang just as I was finishing the feeds. I must have done it myself."

Then Sarah clattered down the stairs and skipped into the kitchen.

Neil quickly told her what had happened.

"It must have been the Compton Beast," Sarah said.

Neil and Emily exchanged nervous glances. Bob would flip if he thought the Beast had been so close to King Street again.

Mr Gilmour arrived just after lunchtime. He clambered stiffly out of his specially adapted car. "These old bones of mine," he grumbled. "About the only pet I could handle is a retired greyhound like Flash!"

Neil took him over to the rescue centre. When Flash saw Mr Gilmour, the greyhound jumped up on his three good legs, wagging his tail in welcome.

The old man was touched. "Eh, lad, you know a friend when you see one, don't you?"

Flash whimpered affectionately as Mr

Gilmour slipped him a dog chew from a packet he'd brought with him and stroked his smooth forehead.

Once Neil had put Flash's boot on over his bandaged paw, he let him out of the pen. Mr Gilmour talked gently to the dog for a moment and then they took Flash outside to the exercise field. Mr Gilmour walked stiffly to the fence, where he bent down and placed a bit of dog chew underneath his wallet.

Flash watched him intently.

"Stay!" Mr Gilmour said firmly, as he slowly walked back. Flash sat down, his ears pricked to let them know that he knew that something was going on. Mr Gilmour's eyes stayed on the dog as he approached him.

"OK, lad, fetch!" he commanded, as soon as he reached the greyhound. Flash looked at him wide-eyed, and then he set off, hopping across the field until he reached the wallet. Flash sniffed the chew and looked back at Mr Gilmour, then he nosed the wallet off the chew and gobbled it up.

"Fetch!" Mr Gilmour said again.

Flash seemed to think for a moment, then he picked up the wallet and brought it back to Mr Gilmour.

"See?" the old man said happily, as he rewarded Flash with a pat and another chew. "His instincts are perfect! He just needs a bit of help, that's all."

"That's right," Neil agreed. "It would be brill if you could give him a home at the Grange."

Mr Gilmour winked at him. "We'll have to see, Neil. Best to let Matron think it's her idea, once Flash's bandages are off and we've done a bit more work with him. If not, I've got a few pals down there. If Matron doesn't agree, we could threaten to go on strike or something!"

Neil laughed with Mr Gilmour for a moment, and then the old man winced. "I'd like to stay longer, Neil, but this cold weather isn't good for me. I'd best get back home."

Neil walked to Mr Gilmour's car with him. Once he'd said goodbye to Flash, the old man got in and drove away.

Flash tugged at his lead, wanting to follow his new friend, but Neil gently drew him back, gave him a dog chew and led him back to his pen.

Back in the house, Neil phoned Chris, who said he'd be at King Street in about ten minutes. Neil began to rummage through the house in search of a book on greyhound

training he'd seen once. He heard a car pull up outside, and went to see what was going on.

Carole and Bob were standing in the court-yard with the family who'd come to collect Digger. Mr and Mrs Thompson were talking anxiously; the boy with them looked very sad and their little daughter was in tears. Emily was there too, her face white with shock.

Neil's stomach sank. He knew without asking that something terrible had happened.

When Emily saw him, she ran over.

"What's wrong?" Neil asked her.

"The rescue centre's been broken into again," she exclaimed. "Digger's disappeared!"

Chapter Nine

"What?" Neil gasped, horrified. He couldn't believe that the tiny little puppy had gone.

"The Thompsons came to collect him," Emily told Neil. "When Dad took them over to the rescue centre the door was open and Digger had vanished!"

"But I only put Flash back fifteen minutes ago!" Neil exclaimed. "Digger was definitely there then."

"Well, he's gone now," Emily assured him.

"Are the other dogs OK?" Neil asked anxiously.

"Yes, thank goodness. It's just Digger that's gone."

Neil ran his hand through his hair worriedly.

"He can't have gone far, Em. He must have just wandered off."

Emily shook her head. "We've already had a quick look round and he's nowhere to be seen. Are you sure you saw him when you left the centre?"

Neil thought. "I definitely saw him when I went to get Flash. He was curled up asleep. I didn't see him when I took Flash back, because I was in a hurry to call Chris."

"Did you lock the door?" Emily asked.

"Of course I did! Chris and I are going to see if the food we left yesterday has been eaten, remember?"

"Well, we'd better start looking for Digger instead," Emily said tersely, as they walked over to join the others.

Bob was trying to reassure the Thompsons. "Digger can't have gone far," he said. "I'm sure we'll find him soon."

"Can we help you look for him?" Mr Thompson offered.

"It's probably best if you go home," Carole said, glancing at the Thompson children. "We'll ring you just as soon as we've got any news."

The family left reluctantly. "Right," Bob said. "We've got to mount a search. I'll check the road to Compton, and you look in the other direction, Neil. Carole and Emily, you search the kennels and the yard again. Every cupboard and every corner." Bob glanced at his watch. "We've only got a couple of hours before it starts getting dark," he said, "and there's snow forecast for tonight. We've got to find Digger soon. He's too young to survive the night in this weather!"

As Bob strode off, Carole and Emily began to scour the yard.

Chris arrived on his bike just as Neil was beginning to search the road. "What's going on?" he asked.

Neil explained as they headed along the road away from the kennels. Chris was only too willing to help out.

"Listen, Neil. I couldn't wait for you this afternoon. I went to check the food we left this morning because my football practice was off," Chris said. "It's empty."

Neil rubbed his forehead. "That's great, but finding Digger's got to be our first priority."

"I know, but at least we know now that the Beast, I mean, the animal, is somewhere near."

Neil frowned. "If it *was* the Beast. It could have been a fox. Come on, you take one side of the road and I'll take the other," he told his friend. "Keep your eyes peeled. Remember, Digger's only the size of a rabbit – if that. He would be easy to miss."

They searched for half an hour in the fields, on the paths and along all the hedges in the area immediately surrounding the kennels. They found no sign of the missing pup.

As they walked back to King Street Kennels, Emily rushed out of the house; beckoning furiously.

Neil and Chris broke into a run.

Emily led them to the beginning of the path that led to the Ridgeway. "Look," she said.

Neil and Chris looked. Clearly defined in the frosty grass, they saw the paw prints of a tiny dog.

"It's Digger," Emily said. "It has to be."

Neil and Chris looked at each other. "Does Dad know?" Neil asked.

"He's still searching the road to Compton," Emily replied. "A young pup like Digger will tire easily, and when he does, he'll just go to sleep. Mum's hunting over the fields on the other side of the kennels. I've looked all over the place but there's no sign of him!"

Emily shivered as the wind whipped up.

Neil felt the first flakes of icy snow nip at his cheeks.

"What about Sarah?" Neil hoped that his little sister hadn't found out yet. She would be heartbroken.

"Safely tucked up in her room," replied Emily. "I'm keeping an eye on her."

"Good. Then there's no time to lose," Neil commanded. "We'll have to search the ridgeway ourselves."

Emily nodded. "I can't leave Sarah on her own."

"We can take the light off my bike and use it as a torch," Chris chipped in. "We'd better find Digger before the Beast does!"

Neil shook his head. "I doubt the Beast would hurt a pup."

"I know," Emily added. "But if it is a dog, Digger might smell it and follow it. If Digger does that and gets tired out in this weather, he'll be in real trouble."

Neil and Chris set out along the ridgeway. The path was icy after so many people had trampled along it. There was no chance of following Digger's paw prints. Neil looked thoughtfully at the gathering night. In thirty minutes, the sky would be pitch dark.

Chris turned on his bicycle light. The beam only reached a couple of metres or so.

"We'd have a much better chance if we had Mr Hamley's night-vision binoculars," Neil said emphatically.

Chris grunted. "He's not going to lend us them."

"But Smiler's a dog lover. We're not hunting for the Beast now, we're hunting for a pup who'll die if we don't find him within the next couple of hours! It's an emergency!"

Chris said nothing.

"If we had the binoculars, we'd find Digger easily," Neil argued. "It'd only take a few minutes to go to Smiler's on our bikes."

"OK. It's worth a try, I suppose."

When they reached Mr Hamley's house, it was in darkness. "Oh, no," Neil groaned. "He's out!"

Chris had a thoughtful look on his face.

"What is it?" Neil demanded.

"Well," Chris said, "when I asked him the first time, he was washing his car. The garage door was open and I saw the binoculars on the shelf."

"Are you sure?"

"Yup. They were in a box."

Neil thought, but not for long. Digger was in

danger and he had to save the little dog. Mr Hamley wouldn't mind if he "borrowed" his binoculars for that reason, Neil told himself. With luck, their head teacher wouldn't ever have to find out. Neil tried the garage door first. When he found it locked, he went round to the side to check the windows. Although the windows were shut, one of them was unlocked and he quickly slid it open. "Come on, Chris, give me a leg up!"

"Are you sure?" Chris looked sceptical.

Right now, I can't see any alternatives," Neil said firmly.

With Chris's help, Neil managed to squeeze through the garage window. The binoculars were exactly where Chris had told him they'd be. Neil took them out of the box along with the instruction leaflet and then climbed back out.

"Right," he said, happily. "Now we're in business!"

Through the night-vision binoculars, the ridgeway was a different place. The land glowed a dull brownish orange, but when a crow flew overhead, it shone like the sun. Neil read the instruction leaflet quickly and checked the batteries, then he handed the binoculars to Chris.

"This is brill!" Chris exclaimed, focusing the binoculars on Neil. "You look like something from a horror film!"

Neil grunted. "Come on, we don't have time to mess around." They set off along the ridgeway, pausing frequently to search with the binoculars for the missing pup. Although they saw a few birds and sheep, there was no sign of Digger.

"Maybe Digger didn't come along this way," Chris suggested. "Maybe they've found him already."

Neil shook his head. "Emily knows where we are. Someone would tell us."

They stopped to look through the binoculars again. By this time, they were about ten minutes to the south of the mile-marker where they'd left the food. Neil searched the horizon carefully, making sure that he didn't miss so much as a centimetre of ground. He'd nearly finished when, far to the north, he saw a glowing object moving slowly southwards beyond the cairn.

He put the binoculars down, but he could see nothing without them. "Here," he said, handing them excitedly to Chris. "Have a look. I think I saw something."

"There's *something* there," Chris agreed as he peered through the binoculars. "But it's far too big to be Digger."

They looked at each other. "It's not a sheep," Chris said.

Neil nodded. He looked through the binoculars again. This time he saw a smaller object beside the larger one. It was difficult to tell because the electronically enhanced image wavered around. "Have another look," he told Chris.

Chris looked. "There's something with it!" he cried. "It's the Compton Beast, and Digger. I think he might be following it!"

Neil was too excited to protest. "It's a dog," he exclaimed. "It's got to be! Come on Chris, run! We've got to reach it before it goes to ground!"

They ran as fast as they could, but the surface was rough and slippery. After five minutes, Neil called a halt, so they could take their bearings. He looked through the binoculars again.

Now he could see both animals clearly. The smaller animal looked more like a puppy the closer they got.

"Come on!" he urged Chris. "It's not much further."

The animals seemed to be heading towards

the place they'd seen yesterday, a hazy dark shape – obviously a building of some sort perched on top of the next rise.

As Neil and Chris climbed higher the mist cleared and the moon rose, lighting the landscape like a black and white photograph.

"It's not much further," Neil urged Chris.

They'd climbed high enough now to see the structure clearly. It was an old, roofless cottage, but the walls were intact and would provide shelter against the biting wind.

"Look," Chris cried. "There they are!" As he pointed in the direction of the ruined cottage, Neil saw with his naked eyes a very large dog and a smaller one going in.

"It *is* a husky!" Chris said.

"Yes, but it's not Tank. Its coat's different. Tank's is much darker."

When they were within a hundred metres of the cottage, Neil stopped. "We have to approach very slowly," he told Chris. "We don't want to frighten it."

Chris nodded breathlessly.

Very carefully, Neil took one step, and then another. Every few steps he paused to listen.

"Does Digger know his own name yet?" Chris asked, in a whisper.

"It's worth a try," Neil said. "Digger? Digger! Come, boy."

Nothing happened.

Chris frowned. "Maybe we should go back to King Street and get help," he said. "At least we've found out where Digger is."

Neil shook his head. "It'd take too long." They were now within fifty metres of the cottage walls. Neil walked forward slowly but steadily, calling Digger's name all the time. When he was within ten metres, he stopped and reached into his pocket for a dog biscuit, which he threw over the wall.

"That should bring 'em out," he said.

Again, nothing happened.

Neil threw another biscuit, this time a metre or two short of the wall.

There was a low growl and then a huge husky emerged from behind the wall. Its face was a frozen mask of anger, its astonishing silvery blue eyes were narrowed and fixed firmly on Neil. Its coat had risen to increase its bulk and it emitted a low, menacing growl. The wild, wolf-like creature stood snarling at them.

Neil froze and then, very slowly, he took a cautious step forward.

The growling grew louder; the husky bared its teeth.

"Try going backwards," Chris whispered.

Neil did, but then the husky took a step forward.

"It doesn't want you to move at all," Chris said.

"Tell me something I don't know!" Neil hissed angrily.

The wind rose again in icy fury.

Neil tried to shuffle forward, but as soon as he began to move the husky's stance became more aggressive, ready to pounce. Neil held his breath and stood absolutely still.

"What do we do now?" Chris whispered, but the panic in his voice made it sound like a wail.

Chapter Ten

Neil's teeth began to chatter. The huge dog stood before him. It didn't move a muscle, but it was poised to attack.

"Creep backwards, very slowly," he whispered to Chris. "As soon as you're fifty metres away, make a run for it and get some help."

As soon as Chris started to move, the dog took a step forward and growled.

"I've a better idea," he grumbled. "*You* creep back, Neil, and then *you* make a run for it."

Neil grunted.

"Try another dog biscuit," Chris suggested. "If you chuck enough, it'll go after them, and then we'll *both* make a run for it."

"I haven't got any left," Neil muttered, between clenched teeth.

They stood in silence, shivering.

"They'll find us tomorrow morning, frozen to death," Chris said, mournfully.

"Shut up!" Neil hissed. He'd heard something. The husky's ears pricked up too, and turned in the direction the sound was coming from. But as soon as Neil tried to move, the dog's fierce gaze returned to him.

The sound grew louder. Neil recognized a labouring car engine and the crunching of gears. A moment later, twin headlights appeared at the top of the rise. Neil blinked and then he saw Mr Mullins' Land Rover skid to a halt.

The door opened. "Don't move a muscle!" Mr Mullins roared.

Neil and Chris watched as Tank jumped out. The husky approached them very slowly, its attention focused on the other dog.

For a moment, the two huskies faced each other, their hackles bristling. Neil held his breath. He was terrified that they would fight. Trembling, he watched for several minutes as neither of the dogs moved.

Then Tank growled softly and the other

husky growled in reply. They began to walk towards each other, cautiously wagging their tails. When Neil saw the wild husky nuzzle Tank's ears, he relaxed.

Mr Mullins watched as the two dogs got to know each other and then he strode up to Neil and Chris.

"Right pickle you two were in," he said.

"Th-thanks, Mr Mullins," Neil muttered, shivering.

"What were you doing, all the way out here?" Mr Mullins asked.

"We lost a pup from the rescue centre," Neil explained. "We found tracks leading to the ridgeway, and then we saw it through these." He showed Mr Mullins the night-vision binoculars.

Mr Mullins frowned. He approached the huskies very slowly. The wild dog watched every move he made, although Tank wagged his tail and whimpered to let it know that Mr Mullins was OK.

"It's behind the wall, the pup," Neil called out.

As he reached the wild husky, Mr Mullins held out his hand for it to smell. It ignored him, but when he then walked past it towards the wall, it growled threateningly. "It's OK, lass," he said, in a very soft voice.

The husky gazed at him. When he moved again, she watched carefully, but she didn't growl.

Mr Mullins reappeared a moment later. "There's pups here," he said, "but they're *hers*, not yours."

Neil's stomach dived. "Are you sure?"

"Course I'm sure, lad. I know a young husky when I see one. These are definitely husky crosses and they belong to her. They're only six weeks old, if that."

"Can we see them?" Chris asked.

"No you can't! She's been disturbed enough without you troubling her pups," Mr Mullins replied.

Neil bit his lip. "Where's Digger, then?" he asked.

"What's that?" Mr Mullins asked.

"Digger's our missing pup," Neil explained.

"Well, it ain't here, lad, that's for sure. Why don't you two scarper back off home?" Mr Mullins suggested. "I'll have a hard job getting her to come with me without you two getting in the way."

Neil nodded. He was too disappointed about

Digger to argue the point. "Will you stop off at King Street Kennels to let us know that the husky and her pups are OK?"

"All right," Mr Mullins agreed, grudgingly.

Half an hour later, Neil and Chris were finishing their story. They were sitting in the living room with Bob, Carole and Emily.

"Chris and I tracked what we thought was Digger following the Beast – but we ended up being cornered by a husky, guarding over her own pups, not Digger!"

"So that's how we solved the mystery of the terrifying Beast of Compton," said Chris, sitting back in his chair.

Emily's eyes widened. "Amazing."

Chris and Neil looked exhausted.

"I think you two deserve some hot chocolate and biscuits," Carole said.

Bob said nothing, but Neil saw that, underneath his beard, his father was grinning broadly.

"Now we just have to return Mr Hamley's binoculars without him finding out we borrowed them," Chris said, optimistically. "Will you help us, Mr Parker?"

"I certainly will not, Chris," Bob replied,

laughing. "But given what you've already managed to do today, I'm sure you'll find a way!" Then Bob's face grew serious. "You two did take a very great risk, you know. If Mr Mullins hadn't arrived when he did, it wouldn't have ended quite so happily."

Neil and Chris nodded.

"And Digger is still missing, remember?" added Bob.

Neil face clouded over. "How is Sarah holding up?"

"She's in her room. She's still quite upset."

Neil sighed. The Compton Beast had been found and Neil was looking forward to helping Mr Gilmour train Flash; he was sure that the old man would manage to persuade Matron to give the greyhound a home at the Grange. But Digger was still missing.

Carole brought in a tray of hot chocolate and biscuits just as they heard the choking noise of a Land Rover stopping outside.

Bob went to open the door. A moment later, Mr Mullins appeared. "I've got her and the pups in the back," he said. "I'm just on the way to the vet's now, cos one of them's looking a bit peaky."

"Can we see them, please?" Emily begged.

Mr Mullins thought for a moment. "You can have a quick look through the window. But mind not to disturb her."

Very quietly, the Parkers crept outside. Tank was in the front seat and the husky who'd been living wild was lying on a rug in the back. She was curled devotedly around three bundles of fur. Underneath her coat she looked perilously thin.

"It's just as well we found her when we did," Neil said.

Mr Mullins nodded. "I'd best be off, anyway," he whispered. "The vet's waiting for me. He didn't mind seeing me at such a late hour considering the circumstances."

Bob Parker shook Mr Mullins' hand. "Let us know if we can help."

"I will, but it'll take her time to get used to living in a house again. I reckon she's better with me and Tank, meantime."

"I'm sure you're right," Bob agreed.

"That puppy farm where I found Tank – when the RSPCA closed the place down, a bitch there disappeared. I reckon it's this 'un. Looks like she's had a right hard time, the lady has. But I'll get her right."

The Parkers and Chris wished him good luck.

Chris nudged Neil playfully in the ribs. "Hey! This means we'll get the money from the *Compton News* as soon as we can get her picture!"

"Oh, no, you won't," Bob cut in. "Mr Mullins will need that money, what with having four extra huskies to feed and more vet's bills to pay!"

Everybody laughed.

"Wasn't that just the most wonderful thing?" Emily remarked, as they went back indoors. "She wasn't a beast at all, she was just a mother trying to take care of her pups."

Emily suddenly stopped dead in her tracks.

She pulled Neil and Chris to one side. "I think I know where he might be," Emily whispered urgently.

"Where *who* might be?" asked Neil, puzzled.

"Digger! I think Sarah might be hiding him!"

Neil and Chris looked at each other. "What?" they cried, in unison.

Emily nodded breathlessly. "Thinking about that husky mother protecting her pups made it all click into place. Sarah seemed really upset when we told her Digger was gone and she went straight up to her room. But when I looked in on her a while ago she was smiling to herself."

"You think she stole Digger?" Neil asked.

"I don't know. Let's go and ask her," Emily replied, as all three of them made their way upstairs.

Sarah was in her room, looking a little guilty.

"Sarah," said Emily gently. "Do you know where we can find Digger?"

"I didn't steal him!" protested Sarah.

Neil thought for a moment. Then he looked Sarah squarely in the eyes. "OK," he said, patiently. "We're not saying you did. But you do know where he is, don't you?"

Sarah looked away. Neil went up to her and gently turned her face so that she was looking at him again.

"Come on, Squirt," he cajoled. "I know how much you like Digger . . ."

"I love Digger!" she protested, as she burst into tears.

His heart thumping, Neil knelt down beside her. "I know you do, Squirt," he comforted her.

"Digger loves me, too," she sobbed.

"I know he does," Neil agreed, "but I also know that you can't give him a home. You're too young."

"I'm not!"

"You are, Sarah," Emily said firmly.

"Digger's had a bad time," Neil explained. "He needs a home where he'll be the only dog, and the Thompsons can give him that. King Street can't – even if you were old enough to take care of him."

Sarah said nothing.

"They've promised to bring him to training classes," Neil said, "so you'll see him every week."

Still, Sarah didn't say a word.

"You don't want to be cruel to Digger, do you?" Chris urged.

"I'd *never* be cruel to Digger!" Sarah retorted.

Neil shook his head. "It's not very nice to hide him away somewhere, Sarah. Digger's a young pup and he needs to be around people. He needs training and exercise and food. You don't have time to give him all that, because you're at school all day."

Sarah bit her lip and then, in silence, she walked through to the spare bedroom. Climbing on a chair, she reached for a box on the top shelf of the wardrobe, which she lifted down very carefully.

She passed it to Emily, who gently pulled back the lid. Digger was asleep inside. Emily sighed with relief.

Sarah lifted Digger out of the box and hugged him to her chest. "I really love you, Digger," she murmured. "I really, really do!"

The puppy opened his eyes and licked her tear-stained cheeks with his pink tongue. Sarah blinked, and then she handed him over to Neil.

"You'll see Digger again, Squirt, I promise," Neil assured her. "And just as soon as you're old enough, we'll make sure you have a puppy of your own."

As they left the bedroom, Sarah wiped her wet face with her sleeve.

Emily closed the door gently behind them. "Sarah was quite clever really, the way she did it," she said, smiling, as they headed downstairs. "I mean, she must have sneaked out food for Digger without anyone noticing. And the way she laid that false trail . . . it had us convinced, for a while."

Neil nodded, smiling too. "She must have hidden the camera as well. She must have been watching us very carefully all week!"

"She must love Digger very much to be so desperate to keep him," Chris said, thoughtfully.

"One day she'll be old enough to have a

puppy of her own," said Neil as he tickled the young pup in Emily's arms under the chin. He laughed. "She's certainly a Parker all right! We can't ever get enough dogs! Come on. Let's go and tell Mum and Dad the good news."